I0678443

SUBMISSIVE FAIRY TALES

KITTY THOMAS

Submissive Fairy Tales

Copyright © 2021 Kitty Thomas

All rights reserved. This book may not be reproduced or transmitted in any form or by any means, except for brief quotations in reviews and articles, without the prior written permission of the author.

This book is a work of fiction. Names, characters, places and incidents are products of the author's imagination or are used fictitiously. Any resemblance to actual events, locales, or persons living or dead, is entirely coincidental.

Printed in the United States of America

ISBN-13: 978-1-9386398-4-5

Wholesale orders may be placed through Ingram.

Published by Burlesque Pressure

Contact: bluepencil@nym.hush.com

ACKNOWLEDGMENTS

Thank you to the following people in no particular order:

Robin for cover art.

Natasha for copyedits and developmental edits.

Jackie, Mark, Cari, Annabel, Lisa, Claudia, Jamie, Michelle, and Cara for beta reading various parts of this anthology.

M for believing in me.

1

THE AUCTION

I never worried too much about the auction. It was what happened to *other* girls. The ones who didn't have someone with pockets deep enough to set them free.

The city officials didn't care what happened afterward. You could keep the woman you bought, or give her away or sell her or set her free. As long as enough wealth had been redistributed back into the city's coffers, that was all they cared about.

I wasn't particularly rich, but I was wise enough to make friends with those who were. My parents had died *out there,* that place that was outside the city and forbidden. Supposedly they were killed by the monsters.

By the time I was sixteen I was giving Stephen Thurman —among others—blow jobs behind the learning center. He was part of the richest family in the city and three years my senior. I'd hedged my bets with others but focused most of my attention on him. He was the only one who had his own money and wouldn't be dependent on a loan from his father. He'd promised to buy me and then let me go.

I'd made it my primary occupation since the death of my parents to be as surly and disagreeable as possible. I think in the back of my mind I believed this would make me an undesirable on the auction block. Stephen could buy me quickly for little money, and then it would be over. Life would return to normal.

Thinking back, it's amazing the lengths I was willing to go to to orchestrate my freedom and avoid enslavement. But really I'd been a slave even before the auction. The thing I had most tried to prevent, I'd lived it for two years to stay in Stephen's good graces.

The day I was sold was a bright, warm day. I stood with ten other girls who'd just turned eighteen. We were fair, thin —but not too thin, with long hair in curled ringlets. We wore a ring of local purple flowers in our hair and white gowns like ancient virgins about to be tossed into a volcano.

A deep and ominous drum sounded in the distance as we were marched around the side of the hill to the platform at the very edge of the city. The local officials called us a *batch,* as if we were sweet cakes or a grouping of widgets. Sweet young women all in a row. Wind them up and set them to do your bidding.

As the procession continued, we moved in a somber line; no one tried to run. I wondered if the temptation screamed in their minds as it did mine. The officials didn't chain us because there was no point. There was only one civilized place on the whole planet, and we were living in it. Outside the city, you were as good as dead. The monsters lived out there. So if the city said: "Slavery, yes, we like it!", you nodded and smiled and then lowered your head like a good girl.

When our people left the source planet over a century ago, they brought with them our past in hundreds of dusty rectangular chunks called books. I was told these books were history but they felt like fiction.

Even so, I read as much as I could about everything from our past before the relocation: plants, animals, technology, culture. Much of the technology they spoke of, we'd somehow lost. Perhaps we didn't have enough people whose minds were turned toward invention on our ship. There had been a time deep in our history when we'd used computerized books, but now we were relegated to scrolls.

The auction was ridiculous and demeaning, but it wasn't far removed from photographs I'd seen of what were called debutante balls on Earth. At those functions, the women had been in white gowns, with an escort on their arm. They'd been on display and presented to society, and no one had thought it odd or offensive.

The first girl was led up to the center block and spun in a slow circle. Her name was Lizbeth, the richest and snottiest girl in the city. I secretly hoped she'd end up enslaved to some strangely rich ruffian, living in a cave out in the wild somewhere—not that our people lived that far from the protection of the city. Of course that wouldn't happen. Her boyfriend had been loaned money, and he would be buying her today.

He'd tease her for the next twenty or thirty years about how he owned her. But he wouldn't really, not if her father had anything to say about it. In her case, it was merely ceremonial.

The whole affair is surprisingly civilized. We aren't beaten, or thrown down naked, or prodded like cattle. There is hardly an air of sexuality to the proceedings at all, as if it escapes these people's minds that if you really own someone's body, you'll probably use it for more than just keeping house. But no one talks about that because it's not polite and clean and civil. And we all want to be polite and clean and civil. It's necessary to survive here.

When someone is bought by a stranger and becomes a true slave, everyone looks the other way and talks about the punch and pie they'll be consuming after the ceremony with those who were only *fake bought*. We know to close our eyes as the girl is led away to whatever part of the city he lives in, and we will pretend she never existed in the first place. At least publicly. Should one of us later pass her on the street, we'll avert our eyes.

I looked back to the center block upon which Lizbeth stood. Fast phrases tumbled from the auctioneer's mouth as he drove the price higher and higher. I could almost see his eyes lighting with greed over what the city could buy when the next transport ship landed. The city officials had had their eyes on computerized books forever.

Lizbeth's father was becoming irritated by how much money he was losing as others kept driving the price up. Finally, all bidders but the boyfriend dropped off, and that was that. On the source planet they used to have these cere- monies called weddings. Just like the debutante balls, they would wear white gowns. In older times there was something called a dowry for weddings. Money always exchanging hands for women. And yet nobody ever questioned it or thought it odd.

So I guessed Lizbeth was *married* now. Because I knew she wasn't enslaved. Just looking at her radiant face staring down from the platform with a kind of imperial majesty, I knew which one of them was the real boot licker. And from the little jeers in the crowd and friends elbowing the boyfriend in the ribs, everybody else knew it, too.

That was when my name was called: "Annabelle Walker."

I grimaced at the recitation of my full name. Really? They had to go there. Call me Anna or call me Belle, but never tread the dark and unholy path of blending them together. I stepped out from the line and went to stand on the center block.

The man running the auction smiled at me. *Smiled.*

Was I the only sane person here who found this all disturbing and wrong? Perhaps what was disturbing and wrong were the secret fantasies I'd entertained of being bought. Not by Stephen, but by someone else. Someone I didn't know. He would stare at me and I would look back at him, and in that gaze, his purpose for me would be obscenely revealed as the wetness dripped down my thighs.

Looking out at the sea of people overwhelmed me, and I felt light-headed for a moment. The auctioneer grabbed my elbow to steady me. There were no women among the bidders. Auctions weren't an appropriate place for women, except for that one time in your life when they were.

I let out a breath when I saw Stephen positioned toward the front. The shrewd look in his eyes and the smirk that played about his lips caused me to suck that breath back in. That was the moment I knew he had every intention of paying for me, but none of letting me go. I looked away from his face, my eyes traveling down to his riding boots, gleaming in the sun.

I'm sure I looked submissive and demure with my eyes cast down like that, but nobody was fooled. I'd made too big of a show of being a complete undesirable. Then the bidding started, or it was supposed to start. There was a long stretch of silence, and I looked up suddenly at Stephen, begging him with imploring eyes to say something, even though I didn't really wish to belong to him.

I had no idea what happened if nobody bought a girl. Was she just free to go? That couldn't be it, because if it was then people would just not bid altogether. No, if I wasn't bought then something awful would happen.

Finally, Stephen raised his hand, accepting the opening bid, and I let out a breath.

"That's lucky for you," the auctioneer whispered. "If no bidder came forward, you'd belong to the city. And believe me, you don't want that."

"Do I hear any more?" He directed the question to the men standing below. A few chuckled. And one shouted out, "Nah . . . that one has too much attitude for me. Nice piece of ass, though. Maybe Stephen will let us watch."

My face flamed as a couple of snickers erupted from the row of girls standing behind me, including the one who didn't have someone who could afford to buy her. Even she felt as if she were in a position to mock and giggle.

As the auctioneer was about to slam the gavel down, a voice rose from the back, doubling the price. I couldn't get a good look at the man because he was shrouded in a dark cloak. His voice sounded like boots crunching on gravel: hard-edged, dangerous, accented. Accented from where? Was he from another planet? From a transport ship? One wasn't due here for another year.

Visions of being taken from my home planet and belonging to some ship's captain caused a shiver to run through me. I couldn't ascertain if the shiver was excitement or fear. Maybe a bit of both. Though I didn't really want to go with the stranger. Of course not.

With every second that crept by, my agitation grew. Stephen looked to be in a state of indecision. *Please don't abandon me to him. Please.* Who was this stranger, and why did he want me? I wasn't unattractive, but I also wasn't the prettiest, at least not in my opinion. I also had a reputation for being difficult, little better than a criminal. Probably the only reason the city hadn't classed me as such was a vain attempt to get some coin out of me first.

Stephen raised the bid, but not by much. Immediately the man at the back countered. People started whispering, murmurs with question marks on the end. I couldn't hear the questions, but I could make a few guesses.

The stranger seemed as if he could bid all day. He hadn't hesitated for a moment when Stephen had raised the bid.

Despite all odds, Stephen countered, but the price was upped by the other man. Stephen shook his head at me. All I could think was: *I suffered through all those blow jobs for nothing.* And then following directly on the end of that thought was: *At least I won't have to do it again. Not with him.*

"Sold!" The auctioneer seemed practically giddy. No one had expected me to go for so much.

The crowd parted for the stranger as if he were royalty. As he got closer, his size became more apparent. He wasn't one of us. Not human. He was one of the monsters, those who were here before we colonized, who had let us live for the amusement value we brought them more than anything else. My pulse thundered in my head, the urge to run seeping into the muscles of my legs. Escape scenarios tumbled through my brain.

The monsters never came to these things. Though we were only able to fortify the city with small, weak fences that could never keep out a monster who could fly, they had promised to stay away as long as we never ventured forth from the one small area they'd granted us use of. Up until today, they'd kept that promise.

He stopped at the front of the crowd and tossed a leather bag with gold coins on the block at my feet.

"Count it if you like," he said. His accent was thick, his mouth not used to forming words like ours, probably because of the sharp and pointy teeth these creatures were said to have. Another shiver went through me, and the tension in my body spiked higher.

Since the attention was now on him, and his identity—at least his species—had been identified, he tossed the cloak to the ground, his need for subterfuge over. A collective gasp went up from the crowd. I felt myself go unsteady again and reached for the auctioneer's arm.

The monster stood at about seven feet with dark red skin, the color of dragons. His face and body, for the most part, were like a man. Arms, legs, feet, hands . . . *claws*. He wasn't wearing a shirt, so I could see his musculature looked the same as most males I'd encountered. Though he was perhaps more defined than they were. I was afraid to know what was hidden by his pants. My imagination ran wild with gruesome speculation. Maybe some kind of barbed cock like a lion?

All things considered, he wasn't ugly. He wasn't what I was used to, but his appearance was strangely and danger-ously compelling. When he looked up at me, his eyes glowed an eerie orange like the fire I was beginning to believe he breathed. He smiled a secret smile. His teeth were sharp enough to end me with a single snap of his jaw.

Despite all my fear, wetness dripped between my thighs. The fantasy of the stranger, though playing out differently, was coming to life. And something in my brain responded sexually to him, whether I wanted it to or not.

The spell was broken when the auctioneer spoke. "Why? What interest could you possibly have in a . . ."

"The females of my kind are dying off. We have . . . needs. Be glad I paid you. I could have just taken someone. I'm showing you respect by paying. If I'm pleased with my purchase, I may send more of my kind here for future auctions."

No one was giggling anymore. I could practically feel the women at my back, standing stiff as statues, in hopes that this creature wouldn't turn his interest toward them.

Every man in the crowd was probably thinking about me bent over a stool somewhere while this beast had his way with me. I wasn't sure if the idea repulsed them or turned them on. I wasn't sure if it repulsed me, but though it scared me, I knew it turned me on.

They wouldn't fight for my virtue because it wasn't worth a war. We'd all coexisted peacefully until now. More or less. And I had proven to be nothing but trouble.

If it had been Lizbeth, they would have charged him with sticks and flaming torches. After all, he didn't have an army with him. He was alone. They simply found me not worth the effort to fight for. Well, fuck them.

A moment later there was a rippling along his spine. I could only see the edges of this change as it moved into his shoulders. Then he had wings, like a dragon.

He moved to the edge of the platform, his hand outstretched, palm up, as if he were trying to appear nonthreatening. "Annabelle."

He spoke my full name, tasting it in his mouth. From him, it sounded like both a blessing and a curse, a sunny afternoon and a devastating windstorm at once.

If it had been one of the other girls, she would have put her quivering little hand into his, her eyes going all watery, her flushed breasts heaving underneath the simple white gown. He would have scooped her up in his arms and flown away. The city would have talked about it for years, embellishing the tale more each time it was told. To some, it would have been a horror story, to others, an unlikely romance, and to still others, a story for a quick wank before bed.

But it wasn't one of those other girls. It was me.

My little rebellions had become so much a part of me that I couldn't give in. I quickly scanned the area around me. The path of least resistance was through the line of girls still waiting to be sold. How would I survive outside the city?

Run now. Think later.

I ran straight for the girls as if they were bowling pins and I were the ball. But the platform wasn't a smooth lane and I wasn't a ball. It was a many-splintered wooden thing that seemed about ready to collapse. In fact, I was sure if too many people got on it, that it would, which was why I was running the full length of it, hoping enough of the men would follow me like some dumb, horny herd and bring it crashing down.

The girls scattered, and I jumped off the back of the platform. The shock of the hard ground shot up through my legs. Then I ran. There was no crash, because no one was following—only the monster.

I ran across the field, scrambled over the fence, and left the city's official boundaries. I was *out there,* the place where no one was supposed to go or explore. Off in the distance, maybe a mile away, was a rocky mountainside. If I could get to that, I would be able to hide in nooks and crannies too small for the massive beast.

Even if I managed that, however, there was still the matter of food, and staying warm, and general survival and loneliness and . . .

My mind shut off the constant whirring of everything below the current issue of running. The situation suddenly felt even more ominous; the sun was no longer on me. At first I thought a cloud had covered it, but it wasn't a cloud. The creature was flying over me, his massive wingspan causing a dark shadow to fall. No matter how fast I moved, I couldn't get out of his shadow.

Then there was a roar, and I was on the ground. I clawed at the dirt, trying to get away from him as his hands gripped my waist, holding on hard. His wings were still out, making him appear even larger and more terrifying. His breath came hard, and somehow I knew it wasn't from fatigue, but excitement from the hunt.

I stopped struggling because it was pointless. If he didn't kill me, I would find a way out. No way was I going to live with this monster, assuming, of course, that I lived.

Then he broke the silence between us. "I knew I picked the right one."

Those words started a faint tremble that moved along my arms and into the rest of my body. What did that mean?

"I can't go with you," I said. My voice managed to sound less hysterical than I'd expected.

"You're already with me. We already left."

Semantics.

He was warm, warmer than people. I didn't know what his species' core body temperature was, but getting cold wasn't going to be an issue with him. I squeezed my eyes shut to block out the images that suddenly assailed me. It was wrong on so many levels—I couldn't count that high.

He removed one of his hands from around my waist. Without thinking, my fingers moved to trace over the fleshy part of my hip, to feel the indentations left by his claws. It had been a hard enough grip to leave a mark, but not hard enough to break skin.

"How do you speak my language so well?" I asked.

He made a sound that may have been a chuckle but sounded like a growl. "Your people have been here a century. We've allowed your civilization and even aided its formation and growth. You think we can't pick up on your rather crude speech patterns? You are our experiment and our entertainment. We are your gods. Of course we can speak your language."

I was offended that he thought he was smarter than me or better than me. Than us. These creatures lived in caves. Of course we were smarter and better than them. It wasn't even a question.

"What do you intend to do with me?"

In answer, he allowed his claw to trace lightly around one of my breasts, then he rolled me to my back, keeping me there with one hand, while the other traced downward, stopping just above my pubic bone. A whoosh of air escaped my lips in a sigh that should have been a scream.

"I think you know the answer. And don't bother telling me how disgusted you are. My kind has a better sense of smell than yours. I could scent your need on the air when our eyes met."

That didn't mean I actually wanted to be naked with him or do any of the myriad things we would do once I was. I tried again not to think about what might be in his pants.

His gaze traveled the length of my body. "You're filthy."

"You really know how to turn a girl on," I quipped. Being a smartass for two more minutes was easier than admitting defeat. And if I gave in to the screeching fear howling in my head, I wouldn't have the mental cognition to form a new plan to escape him.

The growl happened again. "You shouldn't roll in the dirt so much. We're going to stand, and you aren't going to fight me or run again. Do you understand?"

My eyes met his. "I *will* fight you, and I *will* run. And unless you kill me, some day I *will* escape. Count on it."

He shook his head. "I'm not sure whether I find you stupid or endearing."

I didn't bother resisting when he picked me up because I didn't have the energy left, and the field was too open. I needed to wait until there were places to hide where he couldn't reach me. A moment later, we were airborne. A few minutes after that, we were at an opening in the side of the mountain that I'd been running toward. The irony that I'd been running headlong at his dwelling almost made me laugh.

The inside of his dwelling felt like a place someone could live in comfort. It was more technologically advanced than I'd expected, and it made me wonder how such creatures could manipulate technology with those claws. As if in answer to my question, his claws retracted, which admittedly made his fingers look a little odd. I tried not to stare. Those large, strange hands were going to be on me, and weird-looking or not, I'd rather they be on me without the claws engaged. His wings also went back to their resting place. When he turned, I almost couldn't tell he had wings.

With the wings and claws put away, I could pretend he was just a larger-than-average man. No monsters. No drag-ons. Just a trick of the light.

Another creature stepped out from a different part of the cave. Whereas the one who had bought me had dark red, almost brown, skin and a black mane of hair, this one had blond hair with skin of greenish blue. His eyes were red instead of orange.

He leaned casually against the carved-out doorway. "Why didn't you buy two?"

Having another woman with me would be comforting, and I felt both guilty and excited over the prospect.

"This was the only one who appeared to have enough fight in her to remain interesting. And she ran, which complicated things." The other one's eyes twinkled at that. "I'll visit the next auction in three months if you like."

"No, I'll go. I don't need you to pick my mate for me." He pushed off the wall and moved toward me. I tried to back away, but the red one blocked my retreat.

I must have been in some kind of shock, because it had just occurred to me that they were speaking my language. They had their own, and yet they'd been speaking so I could understand them. A moment later, they were clicking and hissing and gesturing in their language. It was so alien from anything I'd ever heard or seen that I knew even if they made the attempt to teach me, I'd never learn it. Maybe they *were* smarter. The machines and buttons and strange technology seemed to indicate as much.

The greenish-blue dragon took my arm and led me toward the door he'd entered through. I turned to the red one, but he'd already left. I could hear his wings in the wind.

I tried to pull away, suddenly feeling on display. "What's going on?" There was panic in my voice. It wasn't as if I felt safe with the other dragon, but I'd had a few more minutes to get used to him.

"He's loaning you to me while he gets food."

He pushed me through a narrow area that opened out

into a den-like, circular room. It was a bedroom—*his* bedroom. The bed was a large, round, elevated platform upon which a soft, thick cushion of the same size rested. Several blankets were rolled up and tied with cords on the floor.

I felt my stomach drop. If the other one was out getting food and I was being loaned for that period of time, I was about to have all my questions about dragon genitalia answered. But not without a fight. My energy and determination returned now that I had a new and different adversary. When he turned away, I ran from the bedroom, through the narrow hall, and back into the main living area. There was another doorway that I guessed led to the other guy's bedroom. I ignored it in favor of the main entrance.

The mouth of the cave stood open with no door. I stepped out and went into a free fall, the wind zipping past and burning my face as I plummeted to what was almost certain to be my own death. A moment later an arm hooked around me and we flew back to the dragon lair.

When we were safely inside, he said, "Now you see why I'm not concerned with you running. Go ahead, run. Fling yourself off the edge of the cliff if you like. He'll just go buy another one. Either come with me back to my quarters, or stay out here and await punishment."

He disappeared down the hallway, and I made a face in his direction. I didn't like the sound of punishment, but I wasn't going to voluntarily go in there with him, either. I knew what he intended to do with me, and though neither of them were grotesque—in a strange way, they were hot—I couldn't bring myself to obey even though I knew it would be the smart thing.

I *should* be in there seducing him, taking the one type of

power I still possessed instead of resisting and having to play
the game at a disadvantage. But I couldn't bring myself to.
Blow jobs with normal human men behind the learning
center had been one thing. This was so far outside my experience that I felt like a virgin again.

Why couldn't he drag me, kicking and screaming, chasing
me down and tackling me like the red one had?

Instead of following him, I crawled back over to the
entrance and looked down. It was high, but there were landings along the way. But how to get down in one piece? And
then where? These creatures—or at least their kind—had
killed my parents and others who had strayed outside the
protected boundaries of the city. I had no illusions they
wouldn't do the same to me when they got bored. I was probably a food group to them.

"He is not as patient as I am. Better to take your chances
with me."

I turned from my position scoping out exit strategies to
find the blue one standing a few feet away. I swallowed
convulsively. He'd removed his pants, and now he stood
naked. In a lot of ways, he was like people. In other ways, very
different. He was broader, had more developed muscles, and
was a color that didn't occur in my kind, but he wasn't
horrific. I ignored the tightening of my stomach. There was
no way I was going to allow myself to be physically attracted
to someone who was such an unnatural color. Or that had
wings. And claws. Not to mention the teeth he was letting
show for my benefit. I conveniently ignored the fact that I'd
had a similar reaction to the red one while on the auction
block.

Finally, I allowed my eyes to go where I hadn't let them
travel yet. It was no stranger than any of the many cocks I'd

had before. There were no barbs. Thank God. But size was an issue. Some of the guys I'd grown up around had crassly referred to their member as their *pole*. Such a description was laughable and a testament to how over-inflated their egos were. But the dragon, yes, he could get away with such a descriptor, and no woman would giggle at him. More likely she'd run screaming.

My gaze traveled back to his face to see the sharp teeth fully displayed in a smile. I wasn't sure if the smile was menace or garden-variety male pride, but I wished like hell I'd better blended with the other girls at the auction and avoided this fate altogether.

He extended a hand. "Come."

I shook my head. "I can't."

His eyes held mine captive. "I need to be inside you," he said softly.

The space between my legs throbbed to life. Certain phrases tripped my switch, and that phrase was one of them, even from an alien being, apparently. The idea of him *needing* to be inside me. As if I were some kind of sustenance for him.

I backed away, careful of the cave entrance. If I fell again, I wasn't sure he'd waste the energy to come swooping to my rescue. I found myself pressed against the wall in the kitchen. He didn't move closer. The idea of punishment had already left my mind.

Until the red one came back.

He entered the cave and put a sack of food on the table. I didn't know if he'd stolen it from our people or if they had an entire civilization that saw to food preparation as well. I'd expected him to fly in and throw a carcass in the middle of the floor. He looked between me and the blue one. And then the hisses and clicks and gesturing started again. It got heated as growls were thrown into the mix.

Finally the red one turned his gaze on me. He growled and moved forward, gripping my wrist hard and leading me down the unexplored hallway toward his den. The anger radiating off him was so terrifying I wanted nothing more than to be back with the blue one again.

When we reached the room, he flung me to the ground and advanced. "Why didn't you go with my brother?" His voice came out a snarl.

What was I supposed to say to that? I just looked at the ground

"Answer me!"

His shout pissed me off and suddenly the intensity of my anger matched his own. "What do you mean why didn't I go with him? Why didn't I just go and rip off my clothes and throw myself at the strange alien guy with wings and a cock too big for me? Because I'm not crazy?"

"It's not too big for you. I know you can take it."

I put my hands over my ears and squeezed my eyes shut because something in his voice was turning me on, and I knew that wasn't the appropriate response. These were monsters that were going to kill me.

He moved toward me and I scrambled away. "Stay away from me. You killed my parents."

He raised a brow. "I've killed no one."

"Then another of your kind did."

"And what would my kind want with your kind, other than the reason you've been brought here?"

"Food?" My voice was small and unsure when I said it because it seemed they weren't hurting for food, and I really didn't know his culture well enough to judge. Being offensive and racist wouldn't win me any mercy.

He laughed that terrible laugh. "I don't think so. Your kind would be far too gamey for our taste. If your parents were killed in the wild by a creature, it was probably the mambose. They fly, but they're smaller than us. They hunt in packs and have no intelligence to speak of. They're common animals, little better than your kind. But they only attack when people are alone. They won't go into cities."

I opened and shut my mouth several times like a fish. I desperately wanted to verbally spar, but he was sitting in a chair now, his claws out and clicking in an impatient manner on the table beside him. It was the eeriest sound I'd ever heard, even more than the clicks they used as part of their language.

"Undress."

I stood frozen, unable to look away from the open doorway. There wasn't a single door that closed inside their dwelling, so the urge to flee, no matter how stupid, was strong.

"Go ahead. See how much worse it gets for you." He stood then, as if prepared to run me down if necessary.

"Please . . ." I said, the tears streaming down my face.

He just stared at me, like I was a curiosity. Like he'd never seen tears before. Maybe his kind didn't have tear ducts. When you really thought about it, crying was a rather bizarre thing for any creature to be capable of. What purpose did it serve other than revealing too much?

He moved a few steps closer to me, until he was right inside my personal space. His claws receded with a little *snick* that made me jump. But his eyes hadn't moved from my face where the tears were sliding down. The pad of his thumb swiped the moisture off my cheek. He looked at it a moment, curious, then licked his thumb.

"Salty. What do you call this?"

"Tears."

"Tears," he repeated as if it was a word that hadn't made it into his language lessons.

"I thought you said you knew about my kind. You know the language. How can you not know about crying?"

"We lurked near men, mostly. Men don't do this. Is it a response only women can do?"

"Men can do it. They just usually don't."

He seemed to consider that for a moment. "What makes it happen?"

"Fear. Sadness. Some people cry when they're angry." The strangeness of the situation had caused my crying to stop. I felt like an experiment, like he might start making notes, which would be better than any of the alternatives.

"Why did you stop? I want to see more of these tears. I like them."

I didn't know what to think or say to that. Everything just kind of stopped, my brain too overloaded with fear and the sense of bizarreness to do or process anything else. Then he spoke again.

"Why are you still dressed?"

Take control of the situation, Belle. Don't wait for everything to come to you. If you seduce him, you still have the power. The self-delusional mental talk got my hands moving to the straps of the dress. I managed to still the shaking enough to let them fall off my shoulders, and then the dress fell in a whoosh.

He tilted his head to the side, perplexed by the slip I wore, as if he didn't expect more than one layer of clothing—nor could he determine the purpose of such. *Sure* they were smarter than us. If they couldn't grasp layers and tears, my money was on my own species' intelligence.

"Take off the rest," he said, his eyes drinking me in, greedy to see what a human female looked like fully bare.

When the slip joined the dress on the floor, he walked several circles around me, touching and poking and prodding. Fascinated. I tried to stop the flutter in my stomach at the way he looked at me. I'd never been looked at so intensely before. Not by any man. Not even while Stephen Thurman had been coming in my mouth.

"Go lie on your stomach on the bed." He must have seen the fear in my eyes, because he added: "I'm not going to fuck you. I'm going to punish you. My brother will fuck you first. That is our way. We share our mates."

The situation moved into sharper focus. I was to be the plaything of two alien beings much bigger and badder than me, trapped in their mountainside cave. Would they fuck me together or just separately? Were both of them that big? Were their tastes exotic? Weird? What exactly would I be subjected to here?

A single tear rolled down my cheek, and he smiled.

"Please don't hurt me."

"You should have thought about that before you disobeyed."

I'd expected him to hit me, but instead, he held me down on the bed, and then his claw was pressed against my back. I cried out at the burning sensation as my skin broke apart.

"Please, stop, you're killing me."

"Don't be so dramatic. I am not killing you."

He'd arranged me so that my feet were planted on the floor, with my upper body draped over the bed, exactly the position one might expect to be in for rear entry sex or perhaps a spanking. He kept clawing methodically as I lay there and sobbed.

The more I cried, the more he seemed to like it. His erection pressed against my ass, as he spelled out words. It was my language. To try to control the pain, I focused on deciphering the message. When he was finished, what I came up with was: Bad Slut.

The words, even more than the pain, made me cry harder. I didn't know why. He hauled me up to stand and turned me to face him. His tongue darted out. I was taken aback by the fact that it was forked, like a snake, but thicker. Before I could ponder yet another difference between us, he was licking the tears off my face while he held me in something like a lover's embrace.

He stopped for a moment and pulled back to look in my eyes. "I love the sound and smell and taste. You will make more tears for me." It wasn't a request.

The idea that I might not be able to please him and stay safe because he'd always be trying to make me cry more upset me enough to cause the tears to start flowing again. He gave me a nod of approval and a smile that might have been comforting if not for the pointy teeth that came with it. Then he went back to lapping up the tears he'd caused.

Inexplicably, I found myself responding to the gesture. It was so animal and primal and oddly comforting. My legs fell open as I unconsciously pressed my mound against his thigh, rubbing against him, trying to soothe the strange ache that had started in response to the power he held over me.

"Stop. You will go to my brother now." He pointed at the door, his tone and posture regal. I could do nothing but obey him. I was too afraid he'd start slicing my skin up again. The pain had receded a little. I think I was in shock. I couldn't believe he'd marked me like that for such a small rebellion. He'd said he wanted a mate. Was this how these creatures treated their mates? If it was, no wonder the females of their kind were dying off. Who could survive their brutality?

I felt a little woozy walking down the hallway to the other room. I stumbled in the doorway, gripping the edge of the wall to stay upright. The brother sat on his bed, looking to be reading something off a computerized screen. He got up quickly when he saw me. I tried to cover myself from his gaze. Despite the fact that I was bleeding, the first thought on my mind was to protect my modesty from at least one of them, however futile and stupid the effort.

He made a sound that was probably a curse in his language, then lifted and carried me to his bed. He laid me down in much the same way his brother had and I struggled a little, the tears working their way down my face again.

He appeared equally baffled by the concept of tears, but though he seemed to find it odd, he didn't ask questions. His focus was on my back.

"Why aren't you healing?" he asked.

"What?" It was the strangest thing he could have said.

"You're bleeding. I don't understand."

"H-he cut me, with his claws." What did he mean *why was I bleeding*?

"I know what he did. It's a common punishment for our kind. What I don't understand is, why hasn't it started to heal yet? You shouldn't still be bleeding."

In his world maybe. In my world, slicing skin like that made you bleed for a while, and I was losing too much. My eyes started to drift closed, and a panic went through my head, a warning that closing my eyes may result in them never opening again. He seemed to sense the danger as well because he shook me.

"How do I stop this?"

I could hear the fear in his voice, that maybe humans were so fragile nothing could stop the bleeding once it started.

He got panicked then. "He can't lose you. I can't let him lose you. How do I stop this?"

"Pressure. Need . . . something to soak up the blood, and pressure." My eyes had closed by this point, and I could feel the slow drift coming. Then blankets were being pressed against my back.

"How long will it take?" He was frantic.

"I don't know, no one has ever sliced my back with claws before." I couldn't believe I could manage a sarcastic sentence. The situation couldn't be that bad. Could it? I looked over to find the red one standing in the doorway, his arms crossed over his chest, observing the scene before him as if he hadn't created it.

The clicking and hissing and growling started as they argued in their language. Then the red one disappeared down the hallway. He returned a few moments later with a cup of some type of fruit juice. There was a thin tube in the cup; I'd never seen one before. He put the little tube in my mouth.

"Drink. It may help." It did help once I managed to figure out the drinking out of a tube concept. The juice was unfamiliar to me, but sweet and cold. The dizziness receded. Maybe I hadn't lost too much blood. Maybe I just lost too much on an empty stomach. I'd been too anxious before the auction to eat.

"I didn't know you didn't heal," the red one said.

"I heal," I said, exasperated by their inability to grasp variant healing times. His study of humans had been cursory at best.

He gave me a look that indicated this was another point in his column for the superior species award. I rolled my eyes and dropped my head back down on the bed. I felt a strange safety in knowing that neither of them seemed to want me dead. I knew it would always say bad slut on my back, but it was hard to get too worked up about the scarring at the moment. At least I wouldn't be able to see it every day.

They spoke again in their language, and then the red one left.

"He went to get bandages. He's sorry he wounded you, but he said he will still punish you. He'll just have to do it without breaking your skin in future."

Oh, that was comforting.

The blue one got on the bed and pulled me into his arms, his hand stroking my hair like a pet.

"What's your name?" I asked, becoming increasingly disturbed by thinking of them as *the red one* and *the blue one*.

He froze at my question and didn't respond.

I tried again. "What do I call you?"

"Our kind believes names have power. We do not share that information with others. Especially not outsiders. You will call me Sir, and you will call my brother Master, because you're his."

Master returned with bandages and left. He didn't even look at me. It was as if he didn't want me. Like I was too fragile for him. Well, fuck him. What kind of psycho cuts people up like that? I didn't ask for this.

"How long will it take you to heal?" Sir asked as he carefully applied and taped down the bandages. A part of me wanted to ask: "Why? So he can do it again?" But his voice was so kind and gentle that I kept my retort to myself. Still, I couldn't process his kindness completely because it still seemed like he planned to rape me. As did Master. I silently vowed I would escape this place, somehow, once I was able.

"I don't know. A week or two, maybe?"

He looked at me aghast. "They'll be open that long? You'll bleed that long?"

"No, it'll scab over by tonight, probably. But it could still break open. It'll still be sore for awhile." The bleeding had already slowed a lot. Probably only a little bit was creeping through the gauze.

"Oh."

After I was bandaged, he cradled me in his arms. So far, this one hadn't hurt me and had rescued me from death and tended to my wounds. So I felt safe enough to ask the question that had been on my mind for the past hour.

"Sir?"

"Hmmm?"

"If I belong to Master, why does he share me with you? Why do you get to have me first?" I somehow managed to get the sentence out without breaking down into hysterics.

"The females of our kind are dying off because of a low birth and survival rate of the gender. They're considerably weaker than the males."

He stroked my hair as he continued. "Our kind has always shared mates because it causes all the males in the family to become strongly attached to all the females, encouraging us to equally protect them all. If we don't know who offspring belongs to, we treat them all as our own. It allows our kind to go on. It's also about respect. We share what brings us pleasure with the other males in our family. It's just our way."

The answer made sense in a weird way, but now I had a new fear which I should have thought of before. "Will I become pregnant?"

"I have no idea. As far as I know you're the first human my kind has taken. Most likely, no. But it is always possible."

"How many females of your kind are left?"

"Not enough to go around. Those who are left are mated. We're hoping they produce more female offspring to balance our numbers again."

His fingers began trailing lightly over my breasts. It was so subtle at first that I wondered if he was just absently petting and wasn't aware of where he was touching me. But then he started pinching my nipples to make them erect, and I knew he knew exactly what he was doing.

I sighed. Where was I going to go? The idea of Master punishing me again when I still had such fresh marks on my flesh was unthinkable. And Sir was so gentle, it would be less awful with him. Or it could be, if I didn't fight him.

It occurred to me that Sir wasn't a sadist. This was just how his kind were. Maybe the females of their species had been okay with it. Maybe they didn't fight biology so strongly like human women did.

A few minutes passed and Sir's hand moved down a little, stroking over my belly. "Are you going to be a good girl for me?" he asked.

"Yes, Sir." I would go along with what they wanted, and when my back was better, I'd find a way out.

I gasped when his fingers moved lower, stroking my sex, pulling back the folds of skin. It was as if he were inspecting me, making a mental comparison to what his kind looked like. I felt so exposed, like an animal being documented while mating. In spite of that, I was wet. Not a blazing furnace of need or anything, but wet enough.

He picked me up and stood me on the floor, leaning me over the bed. I tensed when he positioned his cock at my entrance.

"What is your name?" he asked, obviously comfortable taking the power he wouldn't relinquish when I'd asked the same question.

I almost laughed. It seemed so ludicrous at this moment to be having this introduction. "Annabelle, but people call me Belle."

"Belle," the word sounded sweet, innocuous on his tongue. Nothing at all like when Master had said *Annabelle* at the auction. A shiver passed through me as I remembered Master's eyes boring into mine as he'd spoken my name reverently, like an oath, yet also commanding.

None of that swirling confusion existed in Sir's pronouncement of the shorter form of address. I wasn't sure why. I hated my full name, so it was a mystery to me why Master made it sound like something wonderful.

Sir groaned as he pushed his way inside me. I bit down on my lip to stifle what might have been a cry. I didn't want him to know he was hurting me because I didn't want him to feel bad. I know that sounds stupid but he didn't seem to have a need to be savage with me, and in some weird way I felt I was protecting him. He didn't compute as the bad guy in my brain. He wasn't the one who'd bought and taken me. And I'd seen in his eyes how terribly lonely he was. I wanted to ease that feeling.

He was just so large. And that wasn't the only issue. Inside me, he burned. The body temperature difference came into sharper focus as he fucked me. The heat wasn't more than I could handle, but it was deeply uncomfortable.

It wasn't a long and drawn out ordeal. Nor was it particularly brutal. I didn't come, but then I hadn't expected to. It wasn't exactly consensual. But it also didn't feel as degrading as the voluntary blow jobs I'd given behind the learning center to avoid a fate like this. I shut that thought out because it was so unexpected and shameful I couldn't dwell on it for too long.

With Sir, it was strangely gentle, but not erotic. He came with a little growl, and then put his pants on and carried me to Master's room.

"She's yours now," he said.

"Thank you, brother. You know you'll be seeing her again."

"She's a sweet thing. Be careful with her."

Master nodded and Sir made his exit. It was clear that what Sir had just done had been ceremonial more than anything. Yes, he'd been horny, and he'd gotten off, but it seemed to be more a part of their tradition than lust or anger or any of the other emotions that could be associated with sex. Maybe that was why, even though it hurt, it didn't make me feel particularly violated.

Master turned toward me and my heart started to beat faster in my chest. I wanted to run, scream, cry. But I just stayed on the ground where Sir had placed me.

The look in his eyes terrified me. I've never been scared of another person or situation as much as I was scared of this powerful being towering over me. Even knowing he didn't seem to want to genuinely damage me wasn't enough to calm the frantic pace of my breath.

I felt that if he touched me, I'd die. And then the thought

crawled into my brain that if he didn't touch me, I'd die. The feelings were completely contradictory, but equally true.

"Come, Annabelle. Crawl to me."

A very wrong part of me wanted to obey him like a sexual puppet. That part didn't want to question, such was the carnal, dominant power that flowed out of him. But another part of me couldn't. No matter how much one side of me wanted to submit, the side of me that was still in control was determined to fight. To the death, if necessary.

I glared up at him. "Fuck you. Take me back to my people."

"You mean the people who didn't fight for you? Didn't even try to stop me from taking you? Those people? The ones who love and care for you so much they'd stay silent with their eyes on the ground while a monster took you away to be his concubine? Those people? Yes, why don't I take you back to those people? What do you imagine would happen then?"

I shrugged, the tears gathering in my eyes.

"Yes, cry those pretty tears for me."

"I hate you."

"I imagine that you do. But you didn't answer my question. What would happen to you if you went back? Where would you go, what would you do?"

I didn't have the answer to that, but it didn't stop me wanting to escape him.

"That's what I thought. Now crawl."

"No. Fuck you."

He moved across the floor toward me so fast I lost my breath. I scrambled back until I was against the wall. I was starkly aware of my nudity and the way his eyes greedily took in the flesh on display. My bandaged back pressed against the stone wall, and I winced as the pain flared back to life.

"There is an easy way and a hard way, Annabelle. Which do you prefer?"

He was wrong. There was no easy way. Just giving in to him would be as hard as fighting him. Even though Sir had already made use of my body, it still hadn't fully clicked in my brain that this was my life now.

Master sat on the ground and reached for me. Automatically, my fists shot out and made contact with his chest. It was like beating on a large hunk of steel. It was so pointless, but still I did it. My actions didn't bother him a bit. In fact, they seemed to amuse him.

It wasn't hard for him to shift my body and hold me so I couldn't fight. I cried out at the pain as my injured back pressed against him. He shifted me in his arms. My chest was heaving as I tried to catch my breath.

Then his claws came out, and I resumed the fight.

"You will want to be very very still," he said, his voice quiet and calm. The struggle had left me out of breath, panting for oxygen, but not him. He wasn't even fazed.

I froze as one of the claws moved closer. It trailed lightly up my inner thigh, almost tickling me.

"Address me properly, now," he said.

"Master, please." Proper address was such a small thing in light of this new threat. I couldn't think about rebelling as he tightly held me, with his claw at the entrance of such delicate flesh. "W-what are you doing?"

"If you don't move, not an inch, it won't cut you. I have to use pressure to break skin, and no matter what you think, I'm not that evil. If you get hurt here, it will be your own fault, so be still."

Intellectually, I knew he was right. His claws didn't seem primarily meant for cutting, but for gripping onto rocks and such, for climbing. Despite what he'd done to my back earlier.

"Spread your legs, little slut." His tone wasn't cruel when he said it, more amused than anything. That amusement was starting an odd reaction in my body, such that I almost wished his tone had been crueler, so I wouldn't have to deal with the confusion churning through me.

My legs fell open, and he eased the claw inside me. He was right, it didn't cut me, didn't hurt, but it was so scary I thought I'd combust from the fear. I could barely breathe. I couldn't think. Then he eased back and thrust in hard.

I screamed, expecting pain, but there was none. He'd retracted the claw before pushing further in, and now his finger worked inside me. The fear and desperation had set up an inexplicable sexual hunger.

"Good girl," he said, as I coated his finger with my arousal.

What he'd just done could have been a strange form of trust-building exercise, a general mind fuck, or a display of dominance. Possibly all three.

I didn't understand what was going on with me. If I was to be attracted to one of them, it should have been Sir, the kind one. But he didn't spark that thing in my belly, that mad and ravenous need like Master did. Master completely unmade me with only a look.

He leaned forward. "Kiss me," he said.

I didn't think, I just opened my lips and joined with his, accepting his tongue as it moved into my mouth, thrilled by the strangeness of that tongue. In the back of my mind, I kept telling myself I was going to run away, this was just for now—what I had to do to stay safe and alive so I could escape. I pushed his admonishment about my people and how they had behaved to the furthest recesses of my mind. I refused to accept it into my reality. The only thing that mattered was getting home. And, of course, the orgasm he was wringing from my hungry pussy.

I came then, bucking against his fingers. When the spasms stopped, he moved away from me and stood. "Wait here."

He left, and I heard him talking to his brother down the hall in their language. All I knew was that the discussion was intense. He returned several minutes later. I hadn't moved from where he'd left me sprawled. I had only turned onto my side to keep from pressing against the marks on my back.

He crossed his arms over his chest, and then sat beside me and spread my legs. I closed my eyes while he inspected me as Sir had, only this time it seemed his purpose was different.

"He says he may have torn you a bit, but I don't see any damage. Your opening is very small."

I blushed. Stephen and the others I'd been with had always remarked that I was very tight. In fact, it had taken several of them getting together to exchange stories to convince themselves I hadn't been a virgin when each of them had first penetrated me. Much to their chagrin.

Then Master said the words that started a kind of mindless, groping terror inside me. "I'm a bit larger than my brother."

That pronouncement got me moving away from him again. But before I could make much progress, his large hands had stilled me.

"Shhhh, Annabelle. Do you think I would willingly harm my mate?"

"Yes. I do." He was insane. It didn't matter that my stupid

body wanted him. He was a lunatic, and I had to get away. "How can you even ask that after what you did to my back?"

"I didn't know your kind healed differently. It wasn't meant to scar or damage."

That was the closest thing to an apology I was getting.

He was silent for a few minutes, then he said, "I hope someday you'll understand our ways. I know your kind isn't the same. But you want to be mastered by me, I can smell it on you. If you didn't, how do you explain how hot and wet you got in my hands?"

I looked away from him. I didn't want to think about that, about how I wanted to crawl into his lap and beg him to start fingering me again. How I wanted his mouth on me, my mouth on him. The thoughts spinning through my mind were sick abominations, the products of some psychological damage I'd probably never grasp the source of.

I lay there shaking, wondering what was next, wondering how I'd ever take him inside me if he was larger than Sir, berating myself for still wanting him the most when Sir was the gentle one.

He shook his head and smiled. "Beneath that fire and rebellion, you are so sweet, Annabelle. My brother is right about that." He was quiet for several minutes, breaking the stillness only to give me instruction. "You will not wear clothing here. I want to be able to look at what's mine. You will never shield yourself from me or my brother. You will always be available for either of us to use however we please. Do you understand?"

I wanted to say, *I understand you're a monster.* But the words refused to climb out of my throat. I was too afraid of just how badly he could hurt me if I kept fighting him. It wasn't in my nature to give in, but I had to. For the sake of common sense, if nothing else. I may not have been very obedient or submissive by nature, but I also wasn't stupid.

"Annabelle? I don't wish to punish you again tonight."

"Yes, Master." It was almost a sigh of resignation. He ran a tight ship, and he wasn't about to let me challenge him in even the smallest way.

On some level, it was easier this way. If I knew he wouldn't let me get away with much, I wouldn't feel the need to fight as much, which would get me hurt less. And I needed to fully heal if I wanted to get out of here. I'd need to be strong.

After that, he brought me food. Like the juice, it was strange and different, richer than I was used to, the flavors subtler and more multi-layered. They had a whole food culture outside what we were able to get and prepare in the city.

Soon, darkness fell. I tensed, worrying that he'd fuck and injure me, but it didn't happen. It was so strange, the idea that I was his mate, and yet it was only his brother who had been inside me so far.

He unrolled several blankets that sat next to his bed and made a little nest on the floor.

"Lie down. It's time for sleep."

I was too tired to protest sleeping on the floor, and to be truthful, not sleeping in the bed with him felt safer, like perhaps I could really sleep and get through the night unmolested. I curled up on the blankets as he settled in his bed above me. Then he let his wings come out and draped one of them over the nest of fabric.

I can't describe what I felt in that moment. I shouldn't have felt safe or protected. Not after the day I'd had. Not after what he'd done to my back with his claws, or the threat that existed in his mere presence. But I did. His wing draped over me was so peaceful and settling, that although I still had plans to escape, a tiny piece of me broke off and attached itself firmly to him.

THE NEXT DAY, MASTER LEFT THE CAVE AGAIN. I WAS ALONE with Sir, and although I'd been hiding out in Master's cave, not wanting to face the awkward humiliation of walking around naked in front of the other one, I eventually got too hungry and had to venture out.

Sir was seated on a couch in the main living area, again reading something on a computerized screen. He didn't look up when I walked past him into the kitchen. There were some leftovers from the night before that had been kept in a cold box. I took them out and then stared at the machines meant for cooking, not sure how they worked. It was different from what we had in the city.

I jumped when Sir's arms came around me, and he kissed the side of my neck. I could feel his erection pressing through his pants, and something inside me said it wasn't just ceremony and loneliness this time. He'd decided he wanted me, specifically.

"Do you need help heating food, Belle?" His hand casually moved between my legs, stroking the flesh on display.

"Yes, Sir."

He released me and took the container of food from my hands. My face heated, and the arousal that had been absent yesterday flared to life. He didn't act like he noticed, but I knew he could smell it.

He put the container in a metal box mounted on the wall and pressed about ten different buttons. The box whirred to life and a couple of seconds later, it buzzed. Sir opened the box and handed me the container of food, then went back to the couch to look at the computerized screen again.

I stared at the container in my hands until finally I had to set it down on the table. It was too hot to hold. How could food get that hot that fast? It was like magic. We didn't have anything like that in the city.

When I'd finished eating, I found the place dirty dishes were supposed to go and tried to slip past Sir back into the bedroom where I could be alone. But he wasn't having any of that.

"Belle?" He'd caught me in mid-tiptoe like I thought I was sneaky.

"Yes, Sir?"

"Come lie down on my lap while I read."

I edged over to him and did what he asked, even more conscious of my nudity than I'd been a few minutes before in the kitchen. He positioned me so that I was lying on my back —which hurt a little still, but I didn't say anything. He arranged me so my legs splayed, open and vulnerable to his touch or gaze. Then he started to pet me, his hand stroking over my breasts, across my belly, between my thighs.

About twenty minutes into this, Master appeared in the cave entrance with a cloth bag, whose contents were a mystery. I started to close my legs and pull away. I knew Master had said they were both free to touch me whenever they wanted, but I still felt like I was doing something wrong by lying there and letting someone else stroke me.

"Annabelle," Master said, his tone warning, "open."

I didn't have to ask what he meant, and my thighs fell back open. I burned and squirmed under his gaze. There was a certain level of stimulation involved in being bare to the gaze of others, of being touched in places you'd always felt were private and only open by invitation. But Master's presence in the room took me from mild excitement to a throbbing, wet mess. I knew Sir had spotted the difference, because his finger was rubbing directly against my slit.

But he showed no signs of being offended that he wasn't the one who called forth that strong reaction. He was still reading his screen, pressing buttons every few minutes with his free hand. I assumed whatever he was reading kept shifting to something else when he pressed a button. It made me think about how much technology we'd lost.

Sir's finger pressed inside my opening, dragging the moisture out of me, and then stroking over my excited clit.

"You will come for my brother like a good slut, do you understand?"

"Yes, Master." The order had made me even more aroused, and Sir just laughed and shook his head, still engrossed in whatever he was reading.

I was working for it now, moving my hips up to meet his fingers like some filthy whore, grinding, squirming because there was something so wrongly erotic about Master insisting I get off with Sir, while Sir seemed more interested in a book he was reading. I'd given myself over to the wildness. I guess it was my new way of fighting back. Becoming determined to enjoy myself so they couldn't break me to the point where I couldn't escape later. If I reveled in it, I remained in control. At least in my own mind, even if nowhere else.

"Do you think my mate will be this horny?" Sir asked as I let out a moan.

I looked over to Master, who shrugged. "It's hard to say, but I know you'll find the right one." He turned his attention back to me. "Now, Annabelle, don't dawdle. I need you relaxed and sated for what we're about to do."

My eyes shifted to the mystery bag, and my fear rose from my belly up into my throat, lodging there, a painful little lump. He moved closer, dropping the bag, which fell open to reveal something large and phallic-shaped. Oh dear.

He loomed, his shadow spreading over me like something that was separately alive and sentient, something that might want to do wicked things with my body. Something I might invite inside. "Come, now," he snarled.

A moment later I was in the midst of the most shattering orgasm of my life. He laughed, amused. I knew I was being loud, rubbing myself harder and harder against Sir's hand. I could feel my face growing hotter at the humiliation of Master being so entertained by my orgasm, but I couldn't stop until it had run its course. Until it would actually be painful to keep going.

"Such a mess you've made. Lick his fingers clean."

I didn't wait for Sir to bring his hand to my mouth. I was so lost in the carnal haze that I gripped his wrist and brought it to my mouth, sucking his fingers until I couldn't taste myself anymore.

My body was still humming as Master scooped me up and carried me to his room. He left and returned a few moments later with the cloth bag. I sprawled on my belly on the floor, feeling like a liquid heap of nerves and nothing more. I watched him from the ground as he took the phallic object and tools out of the bag. Then he set to work putting something together.

When he was finished, the object had been firmly affixed to the chair beside the table, obscenely protruding upward and at a slight angle.

He snapped his fingers and pointed at the floor. I crawled to him, my trepidation over our next activity growing. When I reached the chair, I noted that the phallus was a cold metal, smaller at the top then gradually widening.

"When you can take all of this comfortably, you'll be able to take me," he said.

I think I audibly swallowed.

I was still wet from earlier, and though this new scenario terrified me a little, it also aroused me almost to the point of madness. I refused to analyze that too deeply.

He lifted me from the floor and arranged my thighs so that I straddled the metal, then he pushed on my shoulders as I slowly sank down onto it.

The gentle flare and smoothness of the object, coupled with my own extreme arousal, made it easier for me to take in more than I ordinarily would be able to, but I still wasn't taking it all. It wasn't that it was too long, merely that it was too wide.

Master turned a dial and the temperature of the metal started to rise.

I let out a plaintive mewl. "It burns."

He pressed his fingers against the base. "It's my body temperature. It's only that your skin is so delicate. It's not going to hurt you." That's what he'd said about his claws in my back.

He freed his cock from his pants and made me hold it in my hand to prove he was telling me the truth. It was hot, but like a hot beverage when it became easy to drink in gulps, not as extreme as it seemed.

"You'll get used to it."

Then he positioned his cock at my mouth. And that part

of me that couldn't quite make myself go along with the game plan reared its ugly head again.

I shook my head, my mouth squeezed shut. I was smarter than to say anything, because he probably would have shoved himself down my throat if I had.

His claw flicked out and my eyes widened. He trailed it in a threatening manner over my throat and down to my shoulder, then pressed down enough to break skin, but not enough to do what he'd done to my back.

"Open. I won't make you take it all, just what you can handle." While the claw of one hand pressed against my shoulder and a thin trickle of blood ran down, his other hand, claws safely retracted, stroked my hair and face in a soothing gesture. Something in the dangerous mixture of kindness and threat made me hornier.

My mouth fell open and he took another step toward me. "Lean forward and lick. Worship it."

My tongue laved his skin. He'd been truthful. He was larger than his brother. The mercy displayed by not just plunging in and taking and ripping made me overcome with an aroused kind of gratitude, and a bit more of me surrendered to him.

Without being told, I pressed my hands on the arms of the chair and used it to raise and lower myself on the metal phallus, my mouth never leaving his cock as I licked, sucked, and kissed.

At first when I raised myself, he seemed prepared to punish me, but when he saw that I was riding the object he'd forced inside me, he said, "That's my good little slut. Fuck it."

He reached down and turned another dial. I was afraid it was going to grow hotter—I'd just gotten used to its current temperature, almost craving the burn now—but the new dial made the object hum to life, vibrating inside me. I jumped, not expecting the new sensations.

"I reward effort," he said. "Always remember that."

I whimpered, lost for a moment in the taste and scent and mere presence of him. He pulled back from me, his hand jerking his cock, going at a faster rhythm than he could manage inside my mouth without genuinely hurting me. That kindness made me cry a little.

He smiled at the tears, as if I'd cried them just to please him more. And in some dark, secret corner of my mind, I wondered if I had.

"Leave your mouth open." A minute later, I was swallowing, taking his cum down my throat like I'd been born for it. I was still fucking myself on the metal, a second orgasm rising within me. When he finished, he turned the phallus off and pulled me off it before I could have my own pleasure. I cried out and begged and pleaded, my body now so hungry for release, I'd do anything.

He just laughed. "Such a greedy little slut. Be a good girl and I'll let you come later. And I want you in that chair, riding that metal every day, getting your cunt ready for me. Do you understand?"

"Yes, Master."

"Considering our disparate sizes, I won't use your ass, and neither will my brother. Thank me for that kindness."

"Thank you, Master."

Relief.

FOR THE NEXT SEVERAL DAYS, HE MADE ME MASTURBATE FOR him. It quickly became apparent the orgasm was a means to an end. He wanted me wet and relaxed so I could take the metal phallus deeper. Each day he made me straddle the chair, each time pushing me farther down on it, as my walls stretched and expanded, preparing me for his use.

There were other methods he could have used to slowly stretch me. He could have had my pussy much sooner than he actually took it. But he wanted me to fear and crave his cock in equal measure. He wanted to drag the anticipation out to torment me further. It called a strange sort of respect out of me that made me want to kneel or straddle the metal phallus anytime he was near.

Every time I felt that fullness inside me, he taught me how to please him more with my mouth. I got better at it every day, until he could finally finish with my lips wrapped around his cock.

I was hungry for release then, for him to be inside me, but the single daily orgasm to help me onto the phallus was all he'd allow me. I couldn't believe how desperate I was for more. As he came, a little dribbled out of my mouth and onto the ground. I wasn't quick enough to stop it. His instructions about swallowing had been very clear.

He jerked me up off the chair and threw me down on the bed so fast I couldn't think. A moment later, a leather strap was in his hand and it was falling across my ass and thighs.

"Master, please. I'm sorry, please!" I instinctively reached back as if I could protect myself from the blows with my hands.

"If your hand gets in the way it will only be worse. Do you need me to tie you up or can you control yourself?"

The idea of being bound, helpless on the bed, laid out before him while he punished me with the strap was both terrifying and oddly arousing. I wanted him to do it. I wanted him to take one of the cords from around a blanket and bind my wrists together, but I couldn't say it. It was too shameful.

He seemed to see something in my eyes anyway, and I was spared the indignity of begging for something so wrong. He got the cord.

When I was properly restrained, he went back to strapping me. I was crying so hard, begging, pleading, feeling myself growing hotter and wetter. With his power, he easily could have killed me or seriously done me harm, but he didn't lose control. He wasn't angry. He was simply teaching me with the tool I would most deeply respect. From that point on, when I even saw the strap I would go to my knees before him to accept my punishment.

The tears were too much for him. He gripped my legs and pulled me to the edge of the bed. Then his cock was inside me, riding me as I bucked against him. The orgasm shot through me so hard, I thought it would rip me in two. He came, then slumped forward, his lips pressing against the side of my throat in a strange bit of tenderness.

Afterward, he bathed me, his fingers tracing over the scars he'd left on my back with his claws that first day.

"It's not true, what it says on your back."

"I know," I said.

"Good."

After that, he let me come more frequently, and Sir started using me again. Between the two of them I was wrung out by the end of each day. Most of the time, the idea of escape sat as background noise on the edges of my mind. I was kept in a constant erotically buzzed state, so desperate to please them both, to come, to be used by them, I would have forgotten my own name had they not used it regularly when speaking to me.

They'd started both using me at once, one of them inside my pussy, the other in my mouth. Sometimes one of them would fuck me while the other held me up. The day Master introduced nipple clamps was one such day. Sir stood behind me, holding me in his arms as the clamps bit into the tender, hardened flesh. Oh, how it had hurt when they went on! I had no idea how bad it would be when they came off.

Master used a vibrating toy against my clit as he fucked me. Right at the point of my orgasm, he said, "Now," and Sir removed the clamps, holding me firmly in his arms as I thrashed and screamed, tears sliding down my face as the pain from the blood flowing back to my nipples pulled me in one direction and unrelenting orgasm pulled me in the other.

That night, I couldn't sleep. I couldn't shut my mind off. I was wet, throbbing. I'd rubbed myself to orgasm five times already and still couldn't sleep. I was too restless.

I got up from my blankets next to Master's bed. It was late and he slept soundly. I crept down the hall to find Sir asleep as well. I had to get away from this place. I couldn't let them keep turning me into what they were turning me into. Sleeping on the floor like an animal and finding some part of me wanting to be there? It was obscene. Not to mention all the other things I'd enjoyed in their care.

Of everything, it seemed sleeping on the floor was what snapped me out of their thrall. I had too much time alone at night to think.

What was worse was that I was falling for them, becoming strangely addicted to the way they touched me and made my body hum to life. I didn't understand any of the things going on inside of me; I just needed to make it stop.

I could lie and say I was afraid for my safety, afraid Master would forget I was only human and harm me beyond repair, but I wasn't. I was afraid of another type of death. The death of ego. I couldn't turn into that girl. No matter how dangerous it was, I had to break free and go back home.

I had no intention of finding a man back in the city. I didn't want to have to explain the words scarred into my back, but being alone felt preferable to staying and being nothing but *his*. I'd said I would run, that I would escape. The injury had slowed me down, but no more. I didn't have that excuse to tie me there any longer.

I held my breath as I slipped into Sir's room and, one by one, took the rolled-up blankets. Then I took the blankets from Master's room. I dug quietly through drawers until I found the white dress I'd been wearing the day of the auction. I slipped the fabric over my head and went to the opening in the cave. It felt weird to wear clothes. Wrong somehow.

On our planet, the stars are so close you feel as though you can touch them. On a clear night, they light up the sky almost as bright as day. It was plenty of light for my escape.

There were twelve blankets and cords in all, six from each room. I'd learned why so many: they were for a mate to make a nest to sleep on. I didn't understand why they didn't sleep snuggled with their mate, why the lines of power were so severely drawn. All I knew was that I couldn't be a substitute. I wasn't that way. Was I? I was afraid to know the answer, afraid that if I stayed even one more day I'd learn something about myself I didn't want to know.

I tried not to think of the fantasies and thoughts before the auction or how my body so naturally responded to Master's and Sir's dominance. I didn't want to think that Master was right when he said he'd picked the right one. I didn't want to be the right one.

I tied the ends of the blankets together, making sure they were secure. Then I tied the cords around the places where blankets met each other to make it even stronger. The first drop-off was the highest; I was sure of it. Once I got down the first little bit, I should have enough rocks to hold onto and shorter landings to make my way down. After that, it was only a few miles back into the city.

I took the final length of cord and tied one end around a piece of heavy furniture that would more than support my weight without budging, and I tied the other end around the end of the long blanket rope I'd created.

Climbing down was tougher than I'd thought it would be. Blankets didn't make for the best anchor, and the wind kept blowing me from side to side, but I made it down. In some ways, it was almost too easy. At the end of the rope, there was about four feet more to the first landing. I jumped.

Beyond that, it was climbing and jumping. A few rocks to hold onto, then a little drop of maybe three feet. All the way to the ground. When I reached the bottom, I looked up at the cave, a tight, painful feeling in my chest. Was that grief? Was I sad to be leaving them?

If I was sad to go, it only made leaving that much more important. If I wanted to be free, this was my last opportunity. I started walking back to the city, hardly able to believe that soon I'd be back. I wasn't sure where I'd go; I hadn't thought that far ahead. I refused to think about what Master had said, because if I did, I would have stayed. And I couldn't do that.

When I got to the city, who would take me in? The idea of staying with Stephen made me want to vomit. He'd be only too glad to have me. He'd look at the words on my back and laugh and then use me until he grew bored.

Maybe I could find a job somewhere. There weren't actually a lot of jobs for women, but maybe.

The closer I got to civilization, the more impossible the situation seemed. A part of me wanted to go back to Master and Sir, but I couldn't. Getting down the side of the mountain was one thing. Climbing back up again wasn't an option. I'd fall to my death.

What would happen when Master and Sir got up? Would they come after me? Would they demand I be returned? Of course they would. Why was I running? What was I running to? Who was I running from?

Myself. Of course it was me. No matter where I went, I'd never escape who I was or what I wanted. And what I wanted right now was to be snuggled in my blankets on the floor of Master's cave with his wing draped over me, the safest I'd ever felt.

Was I willing to be miserable in the city just so I could hold onto some illusion of a woman I pretended to be, but wasn't? It seemed so silly and vain. And for what? The approval of my peers? Those people who hadn't spoken up or tried to stop it when I'd been bought and taken away?

I kept walking toward the city, finding the idea of arriving less and less appealing. As I walked, I thought about Lizbeth and her boyfriend. Could she be happy with a man she so easily could manipulate and control? Had she picked him because he was weak and she was scared of something inside herself, too? Or was she not like me at all?

I was so lost in thought that I didn't realize at first I was being hunted. Once I did, it was too late. A pack of mambose surrounded me. They looked a little like a type of animal that had once lived on the source planet, called a *monkey* except they had sharp claws, fangs, and small, leathery wings. Their ears pointed straight up, and they had thick, long fur. But they were about the same size.

There were ten of them circling me, blocking off my escape, making strange hissing and howling noises. Their arms stretched out toward me, claws extending, waiting to rip into my flesh. The last thing I remembered was my own sharp screams as they tore into me, and then it was like the lights of the stars had gone out. Stillness. Nothingness.

I hadn't expected to open my eyes again. When I did, I was in Master's room, bandaged up like a mummy. The look of concern on his face was immediately replaced by a type of anger that made me almost wish the mambose had killed me.

He straddled me, his hand wrapped around my throat, his claws out but not puncturing flesh. I was struck with the fear that he'd saved me just so he could finish me off himself.

"Why did you run from me?" he snarled. "You could have been killed."

"I was afraid."

"Of me?"

Was that guilt in his eyes? Was he even capable of guilt? He hadn't acted like he felt the slightest bit guilty about anything he'd done.

I made an attempt at shaking my head, but finally gave up on that and opted for words. "No. Of me."

The tears streamed down my face. I couldn't stop them. For the first time they didn't seem to turn him on.

"Are you unhappy here with me?" he asked.

"No."

He stared at me a long time, then released my throat and moved toward the door. "I'll let you rest. I won't punish you this time, but if you ever run from me again, I'll put more scars on your back. Do you understand me?"

My voice was shaky when I said, "Yes, Master." I hated seeing the disappointment on his face more than anything.

I guessed the only reason he wasn't punishing me was that I was too injured, and by the time I was healed, his anger would have already run out. At least I hoped that was the case. He started to leave, but my voice stopped him. I needed to know.

"Which one of you came for me?"

"I did."

I'd somehow already known this, but I needed to hear it, to be sure. I wish I could have seen him swoop down like an avenging angel, claws out, ripping and tearing at the mambose, then scooping me up and bringing me home to tend to my wounds. I wanted that memory to be able to tell someone. Maybe when Sir got his mate.

A few hours later, Sir came in. He observed me from the doorway. "Belle? Are you all right?"

I felt weak, but nodded.

He came in and sat beside me on Master's bed. He reached out to brush a strand of hair off my face. "He wouldn't let me near you, just kept yelling about what he needed me to bring to take care of you. I've never seen him that way."

Sir's words warmed me. Master wasn't the type to whisper endearments or say *I love you.* But I think I knew. If I hadn't before, I did now. The fact that I was tucked in his bed was statement enough. Though I knew once I healed, I'd be back on the floor again in the nest of blankets.

I was fine with that.

I never told Master I was sorry for running or scaring him. I probably should have, but it was pointless to lie about it. I'd needed to do it, to realize there was nothing for me in that city that hadn't cared for me anyway, that it was too unsafe outside the city alone, and that here was where I needed to be.

A few weeks later things had returned to normal. Master was even stricter with me than before, as if he needed to constantly remind me not to run, that leaving him would be worse than staying. Or maybe it was that each punishment for a minor infraction was really punishment for running in the first place, and he was just looking for excuses because he'd never let it go.

Despite this, I found myself glad Master had bought me that day. I cringed thinking if it had been Stephen. Though Stephen's sexual tastes were far from exotic, he would have made me feel dirty and used, like an amusement, a plaything. I never felt that way with Master.

I was Sir's plaything, but I was something more to Master.

A few months passed and a new addition was brought to the house. Another girl, this one for Sir. She was a redhead and scared, sweet. Someone I'd known in the city.

When she was brought to the cave, I had this irrational fear that though she was meant for Sir, Master would find her more appealing than me. She hadn't fought anybody or tried to run away. She was more naturally obedient, something their kind seemed to like. She just quietly cried.

Sir had gone to the city to the auction to buy her. Master stood behind me, his arms wrapped around me when they arrived in the cave, maybe as reassurance that I wasn't being replaced as the new amusement. He bent close to my ear and whispered. "Ironic, given what I know about your kind, that the redhead isn't the fighter."

When she saw me, she gasped in recognition, the shock stopping her tears for a moment. "Belle?"

I tried to smile to reassure her. If she wasn't going to steal Master's attentions, the idea of another girl there, especially someone as sweet as Lily, was nice. I liked it. I imagined us taking care of the cave together. Being with one of my kind who would understand the things they couldn't was comforting.

I knew Master would have her first due to their kind's familial habit of sharing women and the tradition of giving first dibs to those who weren't the mate. The order had always seemed a little backwards to me, but it wasn't my culture, and Master was fond of reminding me how far superior his race was to my own.

A little while later, I paced in Sir's room, knowing what Master was doing with Lily in the other room. Part of me was upset for her. Them taking me bothered me less than them taking her. She was so sensitive and fragile. I could see how she'd be a good match for Sir. He'd be gentle with her, and she wouldn't challenge his dominance. But I was scared for her with Master.

I also harbored the lingering fear that he would have her and decide he wanted her more than he wanted me. Even though she would still be Sir's mate, I was afraid of being cast aside and living on the fringes.

Sir came in the room. "Belle. He wants you in there."

"Why?" I would have never questioned Master, but with Sir, sometimes it was still difficult. I respected him, but he didn't compel my absolute obedience in the way Master did. And he wasn't the type to punish for everything.

"He wants you to watch."

There were several reasons I didn't want to do that, but I couldn't refuse an order from my mate, so I went.

When I entered Master's room, Lily was cowering beside the bed, her white gown and slip on the ground beside her. She was shaking. Master stood over her, naked, with his arms crossed over his chest. I unconsciously licked my lips. I wondered if this was how I'd looked with him when he'd first taken me. Though I felt bad for Lily, the eroticism of the scene before me still reached inside me and flipped something.

"Annabelle." he said, not turning around.

I wasn't sure if he'd smelled me or heard me. His kind had much better senses all the way around than mine did.

"Yes, Master?"

"Speak with Lily. Explain things to her."

I was surprised by the request. But then it made sense. He loved his brother, and though they shared females, he would never want to damage Sir's mate beyond repair. I understood now why he'd wanted me. Someone who could handle this. Who could handle him. I could tell he wasn't at all sure about Sir's choice or how she would fit in here.

"Will you leave us alone a minute?"

He nodded and both he and Sir went to another part of the cave. I knelt beside Lily and took her in my arms. She was sobbing.

"Hey," I said.

Just the sound of my voice was enough to make her stop crying. I hoped she was like me, that somewhere inside her lurked the same needs I had, and that once she got over her fears of being harmed, she'd be okay. The city had trained its women to be subservient, after all. Lily was nothing if not the shining beacon of their success in that area. She was just frightened, unsure what her fate would be or how bad things would get.

"How can you live like this?" she whispered. "Aren't you afraid of them?"

"No. Not anymore. Besides, my mate is the scary one. Yours is more laid back."

"M-mine is the blue one?"

"Yes," I said, smiling over the fact that she was thinking of them in the same terms I had before I had titles to address them by.

"Then why is the other one . . ."

"It's just how they are. They aren't a very monogamous type. Sharing with each other is just what they do. I don't think Master will be as rough with you as he is with me. He wouldn't disrespect Sir that way."

I sat and held her for a long time, stroking her hair. "I'm glad you're here, Lily. It's sometimes lonely without a friend."

She was quiet for several minutes then she said. "There's no way out?"

"I tried and failed. I almost died."

She turned then, her eyes wide. "Did they . . .?"

"Oh, no. It was wild animals. Master saved me." Later I would tell her the whole story, along with my fantasy version of Master coming to my rescue, the part I'd been unconscious for and could never really know. But right now I had to get her through this.

She looked shocked, as if she couldn't believe there was a merciful bone in Master's body.

"Will you do something for me, Lily?"

"What?"

"Don't fight them. Just submit. I don't want to watch you be punished, and whatever we think about it, this is how their kind operates. I think you can be happy with Sir. You suit each other. He's kind. He'll take care of you. I'm sorry that you're scared, but I'm glad you're here with me." I squeezed her hand, and she squeezed back.

Sir walked in and Lily put her head against my shoulder, making him disappear from her visual field, still not prepared to deal with any of this. He held a glass of something in his hand.

"Get her to drink this. It'll relax her."

I raised an eyebrow. He was trying to make it easier. He couldn't stand to see her suffer even a little bit. I admired and loved him for that, but he never would have been firm enough for me. For Lily, he was perfect. Once she acclimated, she'd never disobey. I couldn't imagine her ever getting punished for anything. Not like me.

He left and Lily sat up again, eyeing the glass warily. "What is it?"

I sniffed at the beverage. "I'm not sure. Probably something that grows in the area. Something mind-altering if I had to guess."

She scooted away. "They're drugging me?"

"Your mate is trying to relax you. He doesn't want to traumatize you."

"Are they going to hurt me?"

"I highly doubt it."

"Are you going to stay with me while he . . ." she trailed off.

"Yes."

For some reason that settled her. We were very different. It wouldn't have settled me. I would have wanted the privacy, for whatever happened to happen without an audience. Lily took another long look at me, then gulped the drink down. "I don't trust them, but I trust you," she said.

Suddenly, jealousy was the furthest thing from my mind. I

just wanted Lily to be okay. A few minutes later, she was flitting and dancing around the room like a drunk, giggling.

Sir and Master returned.

"Will she remember this, after?" I asked.

"Yes," Sir said. "And I'll need you to help her deal with it if she's upset. I hope she won't be. The drug just lowers inhibitions, increases arousal. We call it the primal nectar. It reduces one to their most natural state, free from fear."

I hoped she'd be okay, too. When she came down from the primal state back into the over-thinking state, I hoped she'd let everything go and let herself fall backwards. Maybe that's not the best way to go in life. There isn't always someone to catch you. But there would be someone to catch Lily, if she could just make her brain cooperate the first few times. I knew Master would know how to play her body to make her respond to him. And with what was now swirling around in her system, it made the job that much easier.

Master caught Lily mid-twirl and led her to the bed. She was still giggling when he slipped his hand between her thighs, remarking on how wet and lovely she was. The compliment elicited a low moan from her, this sweet girl suddenly reduced to a wanton slut as she writhed in his arms, her sex frantically grinding against his hand. It was fascinating to watch.

Then he worked a phallus inside her that he'd coated with a thick, clear gel. He went through several sizes of sex toys, stretching her slowly so she'd be able to take him. Each time he went a size bigger, she begged for more, for it to be him.

Finally, it was his cock inside her. My eyes were riveted to him, watching as his body pistoned in and out of her. With whatever they'd given her to drink, she'd completely surrendered, giving herself up to him, her body open and loose and accepting. It was the most erotic thing I'd ever seen. I suddenly wanted to be able to capture the image forever so I could pull it out and look at it later when no one was around to see me. I wondered if I looked like that, spread beneath him, so lost, an exquisite expression of pleasure and pain painted across my features.

Sir's hands moved to my breasts, rubbing and tweaking as he watched his brother take his mate. I looked back at him and saw a strange sort of hunger in his eyes. I turned back to watch Master with Lily, and I could almost understand what Sir must have felt. Sharing your mate with someone else was to them like sharing food might be to humans. Something you did with those you loved because you loved them and wanted them to have good things, wanted them to enjoy the same things you enjoyed, to share the experience.

I suddenly wasn't worried about my place in the household anymore. Watching Master touching Lily, fucking her, bringing her to orgasm, made me throb. It was pushing submissive buttons I hadn't even realized I had, and strangely I felt like I belonged to him even more because he was using someone else and making me watch while he enjoyed a warm, wet hole that wasn't mine.

Master turned toward me and smiled. It was as if we shared a secret. I couldn't tell you what the secret was because there were no words that went with it. It was more of a feeling that passed between us. Sir's fingers moved between my legs, probing inside me, causing me to buck against him, whimpering and begging him to push in deeper, harder.

"You like watching your mate fuck your friend, don't you?" Something in Sir's voice had gone wild, primal. He'd never been like this before, and this new edge excited me.

"Yes, Sir," I whispered.

"So do I."

Lily came then, her sighs and moans so sweet I wanted to slip inside her skin just to know what she was feeling. And I equally wanted her to slip inside mine so she could get a taste of her mate's touch.

I was on the edge of orgasm when Master said, "No, Annabelle. Don't come."

Sir released me and I lost my balance. I broke my fall with my hands, but just stayed there on the floor of the cave, hungry, panting, watching Master—Sir forgotten at my back.

Lily was draped across the bed, Master's spendings dripping out of her and down her thigh.

"Annabelle."

"Yes, Master." I tore my eyes from Lily.

"Clean her up, little slut." His voice was warm when he said it. It was his endearment for me that shouldn't have been so endearing.

I could have played dumb. I could have gone to get a washcloth and basin of water, but I knew that wasn't what he meant. I knew exactly how his filthy mind operated. I wasn't sexually attracted to women, but this wasn't about Lily. It was about Master, about licking his cum off another woman's body for his amusement. The thought excited me so much, I wondered for a moment if they'd slipped me some of what Lily had been given. Or maybe I'd just drank her emotions as they'd flooded the room, surrounding me so that the only thing I could breathe was her arousal and excited energy.

I crawled slowly over, a little smirk on my face.

He just laughed and shook his head. "I knew I picked the right one." It had become our little joke now, and with those words I knew he'd finally forgiven me for running away, that he knew I'd never do it again.

My tongue trailed languidly over Lily's thigh, and I moaned at the taste of him mingled with her and the softness of her skin as she lay there trembling. When I was finished, I looked up at him, hoping he'd use me next because I was about to explode from waiting, and he seemed ready to go again.

He nodded his approval, but he wasn't quite ready for my pleasure. "Make her come again. I want to watch her climax on your tongue."

I was too far gone to care about my own orientation. I could see how hard Master was and how much he wanted to watch his mate pleasure another woman. Lily moaned again, her back arching, hips thrusting obscenely upward as I lapped at her pussy. Her clit was so swollen and engorged from all the stimulation she'd already had, that it was quick work to make her come again. I was pretty sure she wasn't into women either, but her body still responded eagerly as I explored her.

Afterward, as she lay there, I threaded my fingers through hers and squeezed her hand. She squeezed back. Then Sir scooped her up and carried her off to his room to make use of her himself.

As soon as he'd left, Master was on me, his mouth on mine, his tongue tangling with mine as if fighting for a dominance he knew I'd never challenge. "I love the taste of her on your mouth," he growled in my ear, and somehow I knew we'd be doing all that again in the future.

I whimpered, and everything in me became so fluid and responsive that I couldn't seem to hold myself up under my own weight, so when he released my mouth, I went back to the ground, where I could steady myself more easily. And because all I could bring myself to do when I saw him was kneel.

"Make tears for me, Annabelle. I want to see them."

I looked up at him, and the tears flowed down my face. It wasn't hard to cry on command. I was overwhelmed with too much that I couldn't name or describe. If I'd been asked to explain what I was feeling, I would have stared blankly, unable to even class it. But tears were all he asked for, and tears, I could do.

He picked me up and laid me out across his bed like an offering, like a virgin to be sacrificed. I thought of the white dress tucked away in the drawer and Lily's lying on the floor next to us, of how we were like a sacrifice to these creatures. I wondered why I didn't feel like I'd lost anything. Didn't sacrifice mean you lost something?

He leaned over me, his tongue flicking out in that threatening, predatory way, as if he were a snake sniffing his prey. He lapped up the tears and demanded more, which I gave him. He slid inside me then, so hard and engorged that I wasn't sure if the burn was him tearing me or the normal burn from his body heat. Either way, I absorbed the pleasure-pain with a profane sort of gratitude, my hips arching up to meet his rough thrusts.

"She's my toy, as you are Sir's toy. But you are *mine*." The word *mine* sent a bolt of desire straight to my pussy, sending me into an orgasm that had me shuddering helplessly against him.

I liked the idea of Lily being his toy. Of me being Sir's toy, but of both of us having something deeper as well. Everyone knowing their place in the hierarchy. No one abandoned or discarded. A family unit.

"Master?"

"Yes, Annabelle?"

"Why didn't you give me the drink Sir gave Lily? When you first brought me here, I mean."

"I didn't want to." The answer was dark and wrapped around me like I'd fallen again in his shadow.

"Can I have it sometime . . . just to see what it's like?"

He smiled. "Sometime, perhaps."

THAT NIGHT I WOKE TO A WHISPER FROM OUT IN THE HALLWAY. "Belle."

I looked up to see Lily motioning for me to join her. The herbs had worn off. She was wearing my slip because hers was still on Master's floor along with her dress. Master was in a deep sleep, so I crawled out of the nest of blankets.

"You're not supposed to be wearing that," I whispered when I joined her in the hallway, knowing that the nudity rule was in effect for both of us. I immediately felt bad for saying it. She looked like she could break apart at any moment. "Did he hurt you?" I didn't really think Sir would ever hurt her, which was why I felt I had to talk with Lily. If she fought him, I wasn't sure he could bring himself to punish her, not like Master did me. Then he'd be so unhappy. And so would she. I wanted this crazy fucked-up thing to work with all of us.

"No, but . . ."

I knew what she was feeling, what she was struggling with.

"I can't believe I . . . that I let them . . . both of them . . . and then you . . ." She worried her lower lip with her teeth, her eyes wide and brimming with unshed tears.

I could see her blush even in the semi-darkness. She looked away and then whispered, "We have to get away."

Standing so close to Master's door for this conversation was going to get my ass strapped if he woke up. I took her hand and led her to the kitchen where I made us both tea. My nudity didn't faze me anymore, but Lily was trying not to look, as if she didn't want to shame me and thought I needed the privacy. I didn't, but the thought was so sweet I wanted to hug her.

"Lily, what do you really want?"

"What do you mean?" The look of almost-guilt on her face—as if she'd been caught doing something naughty—made the discussion a mere formality. She just needed someone to back her up and tell her she was okay, that it was really all right to just let go, to fall backward.

"Sir said that herb he gave you just lowers inhibitions. It brings out the primal self. That's you . . . underneath the artifice."

"No . . . that can't be me."

"Why not?"

"It's dirty."

"According to who? I don't think you're dirty. They don't think you're dirty. Let's just *be*. Okay?"

She sipped the hot tea and seemed to be turning it over in her mind. It seemed an exciting and untamed idea, as if she hadn't considered the option of just accepting the situation, that she had the choice to not fight. I could see how much she wanted to surrender and give in, but how a part of her still railed against it all.

"Do you think badly of me?" I asked her.

"Of course not! I mean, it's not your fault they . . . You couldn't help . . . "

I rested my hand on hers. "Exactly. So let's just *be* for awhile. Just flow with it. See what happens. We'll take care of each other."

"But if it gets bad . . ."

"We'll run away," I said.

She nodded, her face relaxing. Lily finished her tea and set it on the counter, then went back to Sir's room, peeling the white sheath off on her way. I picked up the slip and folded it as I went back to Master's room. Neither of us were going anywhere.

2

AWAKENING

*Y*ou may know or think you know of Atlantis, but you are probably less familiar with another island people think of as equally mythic: Meropis. Both of these places exist in a world that stands next to yours but never can overlap or cross. Basically, you can't get there from here, or here from there. But I can tell you about it, and you can believe me. Or not.

Meropis is just beyond Oceanus, or what most here call the world-ocean. On this island are three key places, two of which I would suggest visiting if it were possible for you to get here. The third of which I would suggest never coming near. These places are Eusebes, Machimos, and Anostos.

Anostos has no day or night and is covered in a red, cloudy haze. I'd seen it many times from the water when I swam too close to the shore. The place fascinated me in its strangeness. It is on Anostos that I met my Master, Kyros. Only it didn't start out that way, since he's human, and I was a mermaid.

When I was young, my mother warned me, not just of

Anostos, but of land. She said: "Nerina, never go too close to the shore or a man might take you and seduce you. If that happens, you can never come back to the sea."

My mother was on the dramatic side. She believed in myths and legends more than I ever did. The legend went that if a man could arouse a mermaid's desire deeply enough, she'd turn human and forevermore be at the mercy of his lust. It sounded like a scare story my father would have cooked up to keep us all in line. And it worked. On most of us.

Mermaids don't have sex. We'd heard about it. Some of us got close enough to see a few humans do it once. Or a few monkeys. And if you ask me, there just is no difference. We were glad we didn't have to do something so undignified to reproduce.

Merfolk are very private. Although we don't wear clothing, our lack of sexual reproduction makes nothing seem sexual to us. Females lay their eggs in private, then a male comes along and fertilizes them. It's a very neat, clean partnership.

So the idea that a human male could ever awaken a physical lust in a mermaid was too silly to entertain. Which might be why, in my curiosity over Anostos, I swam too close to the shore one day and got caught in a net.

A fisherman eyed me curiously, then started yelling to others to come take a look. They ogled my chest, and I quickly moved my hands to cover the parts that looked too much like the parts of their kind's females. Mermaids produce milk for the babies. That's all breasts are for. No one else would ever think to *touch* them. That was another one of those dirty human things.

"What does the master want done with it? Mermaid fin is a delicacy. He's got that party tonight."

My heart hammered in my chest. I'd forgotten their kind were known to eat my kind. Well, not everything, just the part that was different. The part that didn't look like them. This knowledge brought little comfort, since they couldn't have part of me for dinner without killing all of me. And I very much didn't want to die.

One of them came closer and ran a hand over my fin in the way one touches an object they've just purchased or a piece of fruit they're trying to decide if they want to buy. "Looks like there's enough here to feed the whole party."

I cringed and tried to pull away from him, but it was harder to maneuver myself on the shore. I was utterly helpless, and for a brief moment I desperately wished I had legs so I could run. All at once the fishermen fell silent. When I looked up, I saw why. Coming down from the hill, out of the red haze, was a large and intimidating male, the man they'd been talking about. The man who held my life in his hands.

"What have we here?" He looked down on me, his black eyes fathomless like the sea monsters my kind feared.

One of the fishermen did a lot of genuflecting and said, "Master Kyros, we caught a mermaid. Would you like us to slaughter and prepare it for the party? There will be several nobles from Eusebes. Mermaid fin would please them very much. It would make trading go more smoothly."

I moved my arms away from my chest and looked up at him. While I didn't like the idea of being touched in *that way*, breasts hypnotized human males, and it was either the possibility of being touched like that or becoming an appetizer. I fought back the wave of nausea at thinking of the latter option. And although the former held no real thrill for me, at least it wasn't death.

Kyros stared at me, his eyes darkening more—if that were possible. His nostrils flared, and I think I stopped breathing while he weighed his options. Finally he said, "That won't be necessary, Aric. The menu is already set, and I'm afraid introducing such a delicacy at the last minute is bound to end in mistakes. Cook is already stressed enough. If only she'd been caught a couple of hours sooner."

I shuddered, thinking of how I'd wanted to go for a swim earlier, but my mother had stopped me, needing help watching some of the young in our school. It may have detained me for just the window of time necessary to spare my life. At least for now.

"Then what shall we do with her, sir? Toss her back in?"

Yes, please. Oh, please please toss me back in. I'll never swim this close again. I've learned my lesson.

He watched me, his eyes sweeping over my chest before I could cover myself now that the immediate threat of death seemed over. "No. Take her to my chambers. I'll decide what to do with her after the party."

He looked at me for another long moment, then turned and made his way back up the hill, the red haze finally swallowing him until it was as if he'd disappeared from the island altogether.

The fishermen set to work immediately unwrapping the net. One of them carried me by my arms, the other by my tail—the one near my head—occasionally brushed his fingertips over my breast. I knew he'd done it on purpose. It felt so strange and wrong. What was the matter with these people? How did the females of their kind stand all that pawing? There were rumors among the merfolk that some of the female humans even liked it. We had a word for them. Slut.

I didn't know exactly what the word meant, except that it was an insult and we applied it almost unilaterally to human women. At the time, I didn't know some humans used the term as well, and that not all females seemed to like sex. The ones who didn't maybe would have been happier as mermaids.

When we reached Kyros' chambers, they dropped me unceremoniously on his bed. The one who'd held me by the tail was already on his way out the door, but the other looked on me with dark interest. He stroked his chin, sizing me up.

I tried to squirm away as he moved closer, but the other fisherman interrupted. "Aric, come on. We've got too much work to do for this. Leave her."

He grumbled in irritation. "I'll be back for you, pretty thing. More than one way to taste you."

I wasn't sure what he meant by that. He looked at me for another long moment in a way that made my scales crawl, then I was left alone. For the first half hour I was in shock. It took me a while to orient myself to my surroundings.

The room was nice and clean at least. Paintings of goddesses draped in white fabric adorned the walls. In the sea, we focus more on the deities associated with the water, but I knew there were many others. In the ocean we are pretty primitive; many of the technologies humans have on land just won't work in the water. On land they have a sense of the ancient with their large stone castles and simple fishing nets. But there is also a lot of technology.

From the beach, I'd noticed things that seemed to work by magic, but I'd heard rumors that it was really electricity, like what the storms make. Evidence of their ability to harness lightning was clear by the lights on the wall. Even fire is fairly foreign to a mermaid, but I knew what fire looked like. This wasn't fire. It was a light contained in a circle of glass that couldn't be snuffed out in the normal ways.

Humans seemed to also have very complex irrigation systems and a way to make water move through pipes. Or this was something I'd heard anyway. So far I hadn't seen the evidence of it. There was a shiny black square mounted on the wall and then something near it with buttons. I wasn't sure what it did, but it looked somewhat out of place with the rest of the décor.

Time passed, and I heard music and loud noises drifting up the stairs: clanging pots from the kitchen down below, partying, and merrymaking. The door had been left ajar, and I was afraid someone would come in. But the other side of that was ... maybe there was a way out.

I slid and wriggled to the end of the bed, my arms going out, my hands bracing against the floor as I walked my way down with my hands. I dragged myself on my belly to the door and then out into the hallway. I tried not to think about how this looked. Humiliating. Undignified.

A side stairway seemed like it might lead to an exit. I didn't know if a door would already be open or how I would manage to get a closed one open, but the hope flared inside me that somehow there was still a way out of this mess, and that I'd be swimming in the sea in an hour or two.

I somehow made it down the stairs and to a back door. People came and went near it, so I scooted behind a large potted fern to watch and wait for my moment of escape. But it never came. Nobody opened that door.

Hours passed and a weakness began to overtake me, not only because I hadn't had anything to eat in a long time, but because I was drying out. We can breathe in both air and water. A special mechanism in the human-looking part of us closes when underwater where we breathe through our fins. It's our primary way of breathing.

We can be out of the ocean a long time if salt water is poured over our fins every few hours. It had been longer than that. My scales were dry, and I was desperate for nourishment and for water to swim in so everything inside me wouldn't feel so tight and wrong.

More time passed and then the castle was silent except for the sound of my sobbing. Crying wasn't helping the moisture situation, but I was so scared I couldn't stop. With all of the revelers gone, the noise I was making quickly drew Kyros to me. I looked up when his boots entered my line of sight. His arms were crossed over his chest, and he gave me a disapproving glare, as if I were inconveniencing him. He could have thrown me back in the sea earlier. It had been his choice not to.

"Why aren't you in my chambers?"

It was the first time he'd spoken directly to me. Earlier he'd spoken around me and near me and about me. But never to me. For the first time, I felt like another sentient being in his presence instead of something he might cook later for a party.

"I-I-please ... "

He arched a brow. "Please what?"

"Please spare me."

His lips twisted in a smirk. "I believe I already did that. Were you not present when I announced we would not be dining on mermaid fin tonight?"

"Yes, but why didn't you put me back in the ocean? I need to be in water. Please put me back. I haven't had water on my fin in hours ... I'll ... I could die." I wasn't entirely sure that wasn't his purpose anyway. I also wasn't sure lack of water would kill me. I only knew it was very uncomfortable, and growing more so. So whether or not it could kill me, it couldn't be good.

"I have another purpose for you," he said, enigmatically.

That purpose was unlikely to come to pass if he didn't get me into some water. But I wisely kept that thought to myself.

He was silent for a minute as his eyes roved over me. It almost felt as if his gaze caressed my skin. "I propose a trade. I will let you swim, if you give yourself to me without reservation to do with as I wish."

"You already have that," I said. I was completely at his mercy; my agreeing to it wasn't going to make it more factual. And I had the feeling that my denial wouldn't change my circumstances.

"That's true. But I want you to say it. I want to hear you call me Master."

Humans were so odd. It didn't really matter to me what he wanted to be called. I was too innocent still to understand what he was really asking for, the pact he was extracting from me. Merfolk are pragmatic. We just don't think in layers like people do.

"Master," I said. It was no scales off my fin whatever he wanted to be called. I would call him lord of the hazy red clouds if he'd let me swim.

He smiled his dark smile and scooped me up as if I weighed nothing. I thought he was going to take me to the sea because he'd said I could swim, but of course that was silly. It must have been the water loss that was making me think that way. He obviously intended to keep me, and if my fin hit the ocean, it wasn't coming back. No, instead he carried me to another room with a large, indoor pool and dropped me in the water.

As soon as I splashed, I allowed myself to be taken under, to let the water have me. I'd been so dehydrated that I didn't notice the discomfort at first, but after a few moments, the realization that this wasn't salt water hit me hard. Soon I was thrashing about, panicking, trying to get to the edge and out of the pool.

I won't bore you more with mermaid physiology, but just trust me, the salt is necessary for us.

Kyros stood back, watching. He made no move to help, but neither did he stop me from pulling myself from the water. I lay there for a moment, trying to catch my breath.

"You just said water—you didn't specify what kind," he said.

I glared at him. For a moment I was too angry to be afraid. Mermaids aren't just some legend or myth here. We are an everyday fact of life. Like whales or lobsters. He knew I needed salt water. The bastard.

"Why did you do that?" I spluttered, still spitting out the freshwater, which seemed to have some kind of non-natural cleaning agent in it.

"I wanted to make your situation clear to you."

But it wasn't clear at all. And it wouldn't be until I knew what he intended to do with me. I couldn't bring myself to ask that question because, if by some miracle he wasn't thinking about it right now, I didn't want him to start.

Then he said the strangest thing: "I'll be glad when you have legs. There are many things I want to do with you that require them."

"W-what?" I couldn't have heard that right. He was speaking nonsense.

"I'm sure you know the legend."

It seemed everyone believed in the legend but me. I shuddered with revulsion at what that meant. He wanted to have sex with me. That filthy thing monkeys do. For a moment I imagined myself with legs, kneeling on his bed while he thrust into me from behind like I'd seen happen once on the beach. I made a face.

"Oh don't be that way," he said, laughing. "Believe me, the pleasure will be worth the small indignities you'll suffer. In fact, you'll beg me for it."

"And what if I don't?"

His eyes turned dark. "Mermaid fin is a delicacy."

He went out into the hallway, and I heard him give the servants orders to drain the pool and fill it with water from the ocean. I was still processing his words when he returned, picked me up, and carried me back to his room. He laid me out on his bed and began to undress.

I couldn't think of anything to say now; my mind was too big of a jumble. I felt as if my fate was sealed. Whatever fantasies he had of how we were going to be together, I just couldn't see it happening.

It wasn't that he was an ugly man. Aesthetically, he was as pleasing as the most attractive males of my kind. But mermaids don't think that way. Sexually, I mean. Beauty is important to us. We like to gaze on pretty things and pretty beings, but that's all it is. Gazing. Looking, but no touching. We aren't a touchy-feely race. I didn't even understand the concept of orgasm in the most abstract fashion. I just knew that when someone was having one, it looked absurd.

Even the very little bit I'd been touched so far was so uncomfortable and strange that it almost burned. The only caress I longed for was the cool, trailing fingers of the ocean. A tear slid down my face and he brushed it away.

I pulled back from the small intimacy. "Please, it's not real. The legend. It's just a story. Just a scare story they tell us to keep us from swimming out to the shore. You can't turn me into one of you. It's not possible. Please take me back to the sea."

He pinched my nipple hard. "Please, Master," he corrected.

I cried out at the contact and said it the way he wanted me to. But it didn't do any good. He wasn't taking me back home.

Kyros was naked now, and I had to admire the aesthetic wonder of the male human form. When it wasn't rutting like a pig, that is. I was fascinated by such things as legs and feet and the part of him that protruded out from his body with two round bits of flesh underneath it.

I knew what men did with that thing. I was comforted, at least, that I didn't have the right parts for the sex act. How long that would remain a benefit rather than life threatening, I wasn't sure. The more I looked like a fish to him, the more I looked like food. If I could make my body go along with his plans, I would. Having part of him inside me was far less upsetting than being on an appetizer tray. Like I said, we merfolk are a pragmatic sort. We go with the lesser evil.

Still, I regarded him with wide, frightened eyes because I knew I'd never be what he wanted me to be.

He slid under the covers and ran his fingers through my hair. "Don't fret, my little sea nymph, I can be patient. Your body will surrender to me and transform to my will in time."

For the tiniest fraction of a moment I believed him because I felt something when he said those words. Something inside me that twitched an almost imperceptible amount. But then it was gone as quickly as it had come, and I thought I'd imagined it. Or maybe it was just fear.

His fingers traveled across my body, over my face, my arms, my belly, and my hip where it flared into aquamarine fin. He stroked over the fin, all the way to the tail—only the way he touched me wasn't like food, like the fishermen. It was like something else.

I closed my eyes and breathed slowly, trying to assimilate the feel of flesh against flesh. It was strange, disconcerting, uncomfortable. Not completely unpleasant. But it wasn't anything that was going to make me turn human, not even if the legend were true.

Then his hands went to my breasts, the one area he'd skipped over in his calm exploration of his prize. He stroked them for a moment, and my face heated. For the first time, I felt embarrassment over my breasts being exposed, because the way he was touching them let me know that every other male who had seen them had wanted to touch them in this way, too. It was too personal and intimate. It made me long for clothing to cover up, to hide.

A few moments of this touching passed, and then his mouth descended on me, suckling at my nipple. I'd had no young so I'd never had a mouth latched onto my breast like that. I was quite sure other mermaids didn't experience what I was now experiencing. There was that light, internal twitch again. It flared into a small, steady flame and drew a gasp from me. Then it flickered out like a ghost.

His voice murmured and reverberated against my flesh. "I've always wanted a woman I could build from the ground up. I've thought about turning one of your kind for a long time now. I couldn't believe my luck when you washed ashore. This is my best birthday."

He sounded almost kind when he said it, and I wanted to believe him. The party must have been a celebration of his birth, and I was the unexpected gift that had come in with the tide, wrapped in black netting.

It occurred to me that maybe he'd never wanted to dine on mermaid fin. Perhaps it was all bluster and show. I'd heard that about human males. The seagulls liked to gossip, and I always got my fair share of intriguing human information that way.

Kyros laid his head on my chest, holding me against him. Something caused me to reach out to him. I don't know why, but I ran my fingers through his hair. Some part of me tried to believe that if I could make him care for me, he wouldn't kill me when I couldn't respond and change into a human. Maybe he'd care enough to return me to the sea, or if not that, at least not harm me here.

"Master?" I knew it was pointless to address him any other way. And if I wanted something, approaching him with any other word would work against me.

"Yes ... " he paused, at a loss. "What *is* your name, by the way?"

"Nerina."

"Nerina. I like it."

I hesitated a moment, then plunged on, my voice quiet, a whisper. "Will you please take me back to the water?"

"When the pool is ready for you, yes. You can sleep there until you don't need it anymore."

I didn't argue. I was always going to need it because I was always going to be a mermaid. His fervent belief wouldn't change reality.

Time began to hold no meaning as he held me, as if his skin against mine could bring something new inside me to life. Slowly, he ran his hands over me until I began to relax and just let it happen, just feel. Then his lips went everywhere his hands had been. I shuddered as his warm, wet tongue moved up the side of my throat. Then the licking turned to kisses that moved across my jawline to my lips.

His tongue speared inside my mouth, and I jerked away, surprised. Then a dark connection formed in my mind. I might not have all the proper parts for him to get inside me, but his tongue darting in and out of my mouth made me aware of what else he could put in there. I started to struggle.

On land, my fin was a confining bondage, making me feel wrapped tight like a mummy. It had never felt unnatural before, like something that shouldn't be there. But now all it did was close off my escape even further.

Kyros pulled away, giving me a hard, displeased look that made me wither and sink back against the blankets.

"Don't resist me. I'm going to mold you into my vessel, and you're going to thank me for it with obedience."

Twitch.

The way he spoke was offensive. I'd never been treated in this manner before. It was as if I were a thing to him. A toy or a pet. And yet, when he did, that little flicker happened. I wanted to feel that flicker again and see where it would go, what it might turn into.

"Do you understand?"

He looked ready to deliver more pain, so I quickly answered, "Yes, Master."

He nodded and went back to kissing me. I was beyond the discomfort of being touched. After the way the pinching felt when he'd intentionally brought me pain, everything else started to feel good by comparison. I ignored the voice in my mind that said I was starting to welcome his hands and mouth. That voice sounded too much like a human female. Like a slut.

We were interrupted a few moments later by a knock on the door. "Master Kyros, the pool is ready for her."

I TENSED WHEN HE DROPPED ME INTO THE WATER AGAIN, NOT quite convinced I wouldn't be met with that awful, chemically altered freshwater. My muscles unclenched as I realized it was part of the ocean. I swam around in little circles and surged out of the water like a dolphin before splashing back in again.

I knew Kyros was watching me, but I didn't care. Let the human watch the only real pleasure he could ever give me. I wondered if he would become jealous of the water, how it made me come to life and caused bliss to spread across my features. Bliss he would never be capable of with his own hands. I was sure of it.

I looked up to find him standing over me. He was still naked, without a shred of modesty. Maybe like me in that way. Or like I'd been before, when having bare breasts was innocent and natural. Certainly nothing dirty or sexual. His legs were solid and unmoving like a tree.

My gaze panned up. His arms were crossed over his chest. Finally my eyes reached his face. There was an amused grin there.

"Enjoy your fin while you have it, Nerina. I will seduce, and I will win. Rest well." With that pronouncement, he left. I tried not to watch the sinewy muscles bunch and release as he went away. It seemed such curiosity would only lead to the thing I feared losing the most.

His parting words took a bit of joy out of swimming. I sank beneath the water, trying to imagine that I was back in the sea. The real sea, not this artificial sea that had been created with only a small piece of the ocean. I'm not sure if I was crying. It's impossible to tell when underwater. But I felt like I must be.

It was at that moment that I finally got out of my own head to realize my family would be missing me. They might never know what happened. They might imagine all sorts of awful things, like a shark or sea monster attack. I was known for wandering off in places I shouldn't go. Even so, my mother would never believe, after her warnings about men, that I would be on land, the captive of one.

What if Kyros won? What if the legend was real and he could make my body feel whatever it had to feel to make the transformation happen? I looked down and watched my fin fluttering about in the water. How could he take that from me? How could I let him?

I swam to the deepest corner of the pool and curled up to sleep. The next day I would find a way to get him to release me and go back to my life in the ocean.

That night as I slept I saw pictures in my mind. The images were brief, small, like the embryonic form of something that would grow larger over time. It was just a quick snippet of him and me, and I had legs, which were draped over his shoulders. It was vulgar to me. And yet ...

Twitch.

I woke immediately, fear causing me to lose the fuzzy vision. My fin was still there, and I was alone. But the images haunted me. Not only because of the content, but because I'd seen them at all. It was so real.

I swam laps back and forth in the pool, as if my fin might

somehow split in two to form legs at any moment. I felt that if I just kept swimming, I could stay a mermaid forever. It was what I wanted most. Wasn't it? I finally drifted, exhausted, back to my corner. I wrapped my fin around me and slept, unmolested by further disturbances.

Morning came too quickly and I sensed a presence beside the pool. I opened my eyes and swam to the surface. Kyros still wasn't clothed. He sat on the concrete edge and dropped his legs in.

I'm not sure why I'd thought of the pool as a safe haven from him. It wasn't that deep, and surely he'd been in it before. Why else would he have it? To keep mermaid pets? Definitely not if it hadn't been filled with seawater.

He lowered himself the rest of the way in and started to do laps. I was surprised he could swim, and so well. I could understand why they'd avoid it in the ocean. With the sharks and sea monsters, it's a lot to deal with for someone who doesn't have to for survival. Or maybe they sometimes swam close to land, and I hadn't noticed them.

I watched his legs kicking out as he smoothly traveled through the water. Finally I surfaced to watch from above.

After about twenty minutes of laps he stopped and stood in the shallow end of the pool, the water coming up to just below his pecs.

"I might keep the ocean water. It's refreshing." He ran his hands through his hair, and I closed my eyes.

After last night and the way he'd touched me, the way I'd been at his full command, something felt different. And that feeling seemed like a dark threat.

As if answering the confusing swirl of thoughts in my head, he said, "See, Nerina? You'll still be able to swim."

"It's not the same." I wouldn't be able to breathe underwater. I wouldn't be able to swim out deep to sea and go underneath it for miles and miles. I'd never be able to go home. For a moment, I fantasized about pushing him under, drowning him. But it was only a fantasy. It wouldn't free me. His servants would probably cook me for dinner in retribution. I wasn't strong enough to overpower him anyway.

Fantasizing made me remember what had happened the night before. The images. "Were you here last night? After I was asleep?"

His eyes narrowed. "Address me properly."

"I'm sorry, Master. But were you?"

Kyros shook his head. "No, Nerina. I was asleep. Why?"

I considered not even bringing it up. Whatever it was somehow hadn't been real. Maybe it had just been my imagination. But imagination had never been so vivid before.

"Nerina?"

"I saw you and me. But I had legs. It was so real. Then I opened my eyes in the pool, and you were gone and my fin was intact."

He chuckled. "Don't mermaids dream?"

"Dream?" It was the first time I'd heard the word for what had happened while I slept.

"Humans do it all the time."

That statement made me cold. First the twitch, now the brief *dream*. And to make matters worse, it had been about him and me and the thing my kind didn't do. Sex. Even the word made me shudder in discomfort. No, I was never going to become like that. I wouldn't allow it to happen.

"Master, please. You've had your fun; return me to my family. Let me go."

He swam toward me like a shark, his eyes filled with

purpose. I was faster, so I kept eluding him. Finally he stopped swimming, realizing the futility of the chase.

"Nerina, if you don't come to me right now, I'll order the pool drained. Then we'll see who is the fastest."

Fear quickened my heart, starting a flurry of palpitations. I believed him. Short term I knew there would be some type of pain for not obeying. Long term, I was afraid he wouldn't refill the pool. I didn't want to awaken the part of him that might be cruel and do awful things to me, so I slowly swam to where he stood waiting in the shallow end.

He wrapped his arms around me, lifting me when I reached him, holding me steady since I had no feet to stand. The fingers of one hand stroked through my tangled, wet hair.

"Does your kind never leave their family?"

I shook my head. What did he mean leave our family? We lived together, all of us in a large school, like fish. I should have figured out humans didn't do that. I just assumed everyone was somehow part of the same family here. Obviously not.

"Well, my kind does. Women often leave their families to go with their husband. Sometimes hundreds or thousands of miles away. Sometimes they never see them again."

The revelation was more than I could assimilate. "That's awful. What is *wrong* with your kind?"

He silenced my protests and railings with a kiss. I knew what he was doing. I might not know everything about their culture, but I did know one thing: if he could take my fin away, I'd have no choice but to stay with him. Then he wouldn't be the bad guy. It would be my own body that had betrayed me.

I sobbed into his mouth because I was afraid he was right.

I feared he was awakening me from a long slumber caused by all my years living deep in the ocean, where maybe we didn't dream because it was all a dream down there. Everything from my time in the sea somehow felt unreal and fuzzy in his arms. I couldn't think with his mouth moving over mine like that. The way he held me. His possessive, proprietary kiss.

He made a sound against my mouth that for a split second almost undid me. It made me melt against him. My breasts, still wet from the pool, pressed against his equally damp chest.

Twitch.

If I didn't fight these feelings I might lose myself to him. I'd thought the legends weren't true, but with the feeling he was awakening in me, paired with the dream, I was no longer so confident. I told myself I still wanted to get away, but one thing gave me pause.

If I went back to my family they would love me, but they wouldn't touch me in any way. Somehow in the space of one day, I'd grown almost fond of my Master's careful touch. Now that I'd experienced it, I wasn't sure I wanted to go back to a place where no one would ever hold me.

My kind would admire me for the beauty we all had, but no man would sear me with his gaze in the way Kyros did every time he looked at me. My only lover would be the sea itself. Was that enough?

He broke the kiss. "Are you hungry?"

I flushed because something had twisted the tiniest bit in my mind. Hungry. Was I hungry? Yes, but not for food. I quickly shook myself out of his spell and pulled away. He let me go and I swam around the pool, reassuring myself I still had my fin.

As he climbed out, I tried not to watch the water rolling

down his perfect, nude form. I tried not to be curious or think about the thing that would take away a major part of my identity. Mermaids are very proud of who and what we are. To be stripped of that, to become one of these human animals—it was more than I could stand.

I swam laps again, even though I was starving and all the swimming only made me feel weaker. He returned a few moments later, fully clothed—thank the gods. He had a pail of fish and tossed them into the pool. They were still alive, which was good, because that was how we ate them. Bigger fish eat little fish, and in a sense, mermaids are *bigger fish*.

I was surprised he knew what we ate. Humans are always romanticizing us, making us into a type of fantasy that would never eat a live fish. I guess that's not attractive to them. I knew Kyros in many ways saw me as the fantasy because of his belief in the legend and his determination to turn a mermaid. I still didn't understand his build-a-woman-from-the-ground-up statement.

He brought his breakfast in and sat beside the pool to eat. I didn't know what he was eating, but he offered me some, feeding me from his hand. The act was so intimate, his fingers brushing over my lips, the gentle caring in the act. It created a new feeling. Not the twitch, but a kind of warmth that suffused my entire being.

The first thing was red and sort of triangular. The flavor burst over my tongue.

"It's sweet. What is it?"

"Fruit. Specifically a strawberry. And this is a grape." He pressed the oblong purple fruit into my mouth, his finger lingering for just a moment longer than was necessary. When he pulled his hand away and I bit down, I was surprised by the sudden burst of juice. More than the other fruit. "Now try this one, it's an orange wedge."

The last was sweet, but then bitter and rubbery. I spit it out.

"Oh, no, Nerina, not the rind." The next orange, he peeled the bad part off for me. This time it was sweet and perfect all the way through.

Then he handed me a small cube that was yellow in color and firm, but also a bit soft. "This is cheese."

I must admit, the contrast of the cheese and the fruit was exquisite. And for just a small moment, I wasn't homesick. This new world of flavors made me dread going back to eating fish and seaweed. It was as if my taste buds were awakened to new, exotic things I'd never known existed, and my former diet paled in comparison.

There was also meat on his plate of some sort, cooked meat. I didn't know how I felt about that, but he didn't offer me any. Perhaps because I'd already had fish. When we were both satisfied, he scooped me up out of the water and took me to his chambers again.

A nervous flutter started low in my stomach, right above my fin, as we entered his room. He laid down a type of absorbent cloth he called a bath towel on the bed and used it to dry me so I wouldn't get the bed wet with seawater.

The quick heartbeat started again as he settled in next to me, his hand starting that gentle stroking, the touches that were starting to feel nice and welcome. Especially after he'd shared his breakfast with me.

I let out a soft sigh as the pads of his fingertips brushed over my nipple. He kept touching and stroking until they were hardened points. The effect was accompanied by the twitch again, and as he smiled at me, it turned into a flicker and then the beginnings of a flame.

A moment later the door opened, and a portly older woman walked in, smothering the flame. "Master Kyros, I was wondering if you wanted the new linens in the closet or in here." She looked up from the folded bundle in her arms. "Oh, excuse me, sir, I do apologize. I'll come back another time."

"Leave the linens on the chair," Kyros said, not taking his eyes from me.

He was unfazed by his own nudity, even in the presence of this disapproving matronly woman. I, on the other hand, had developed an extreme case of modesty. The look of distaste the woman gave me, as if I were something dirty and wrong, had me rushing to cover myself, but Kyros gripped my wrist, stopping me.

The servant put the linens down, then sort of ... lingered.

"That will be all, Estella."

She flushed and left us alone, shutting the door behind her. Kyros got up and locked the door, an act for which I was deeply grateful. My misgivings must have shown on my face, because he said, "Don't worry about her. She's just an old woman who doesn't remember what it's like. Or else she's merely jealous her time has passed."

He went back to the stroking and gentle caresses. Then his mouth was on mine, a full-on assault as if he would accept nothing but my utter surrender. I whimpered against him, returning the kiss with equal intensity. I'm not sure if this intensity I gave him was my own fear manifesting as an action I could take to appease him, or if there was something new growing inside me. A new curiosity and hunger.

After a while of this, he pulled away and lay back on the

bed. Without a word, he guided my hands over his body, making me stroke the hard planes of his chest, the musculature of his arms, his face, his eyelids, his hair, his thighs, and finally what was between his legs. When I first touched it, my instinct was to pull back. It stood erect and hard, but the skin was so soft, softer than anything I'd ever felt.

He helped me close my hand around it and guided me to pump up and down. I blushed, because I knew what I was doing was something deeply intimate and a simulation of the sex act, but I was so fascinated by the whole thing that I kept going, not listening to the twitch and flicker as it started again, not realizing that each moment in an intimate embrace with Kyros moved me that much closer to becoming truly his.

He urged me on harder and harder until finally something happened. It was like an explosion. I couldn't hear it, except for the low, masculine groan, but I could see it as something shot out of him, coming to rest on his stomach. Then that frightening and fascinating part of him went limp, as if it were tired.

While he seemed to be satisfied, I was far from it. I had a new need forming that I didn't have a word for. It felt like being itchy on the inside with no way to reach it to satisfy the feeling. It was uncomfortable and scary, and I wished I understood humanity more, because it made me feel lonely.

His lids dropped a little, a smile spreading across his face, his features relaxed. Then he ran a finger through the liquid on his stomach and brought it to my lips.

"Taste me, Nerina."

His intensity scared me, but the command made my skin heat up. I tried to imagine one of my kind asking me to do something so intimate. Even if they had the right equipment,

I couldn't fathom such an exchange ever happening. I couldn't even imagine being fed by a male, or holding hands.

But for Kyros, this request was as natural as breathing. I inched closer, wondering if just tasting him could somehow put out the flame burning through me. I closed my mouth around his finger and sucked the liquid off. Salty. Primal. It was like the sea. Somewhere deep in my mind, I knew he could be my new ocean.

It was a heady and terrifying thought, that one person could loom so large and be so much to me. I didn't want to accept its truth.

He gently grasped the back of my neck, urging me forward to lick it straight off his stomach. As my tongue ran over him, he massaged my neck and played with my hair. Something about the twitch changed until it became a deep throb. I felt as if my fin were electrified. The pulsing feeling was too frightening, too much. I pulled away.

"No, please, Master."

His eyes narrowed, disapproval creasing his brow, and I knew he must be thinking about punishing me, but in the end he merely used the towel I'd been reclining on to wipe his stomach clean.

"All right, Nerina. I'll slow down. But you can't have your own pleasure until you surrender to me."

He nestled me against him and rubbed my back for a little while, then took me to the pool.

A few weeks passed like this, and I knew he was growing impatient. At night my dreams became longer and more vivid. In the dreams, when he took me, I could feel that throb start again. Every time, I woke up before anything happened, before I could find out how that throb ended and what it became.

He spent endless amounts of time stroking me, kissing me, nibbling on my neck, suckling my breasts, having me touch and stroke him. Each time the feelings that had started to grow got stronger, scarier. They felt like a violent storm brewing inside me, like a disaster poised and ready to strike.

At each meal he fed me from his plate, his fingers lingering in my mouth so I could suck off the juices from the food, whether it was fruit or meat. Slowly, live fish became distasteful to me. Soon I was eating meat like him and drinking wine.

The wine made my head a little fuzzy, made me braver. It made me crave him inside me. Such a weird thing to crave. I only understood the concept on the most basic level. If you drew me a diagram I would have gotten it, but only as a theoretical principle. Not as a living reality.

I knew he was plying me with alcohol to speed the process, to turn me into something he could take his full pleasure inside.

One night, a little drunk, I lay in his bed while the servants drained and refilled the pool with fresh seawater. He started touching and stroking me.

"Master?"

"Yes, Nerina?"

"If the legend isn't real, are you going to kill me?" It was the thought that lurked deep inside me, always driving a little buzz of anxiety, making me try to please him a little more to hold off my fate.

He waited a long time before answering, his voice distant and sad when he finally did. "No. I'll give it a little more time, and then I'll return you to your home. Maybe you belong out there. Perhaps it was foolish to think you could ever be mine in that way."

Home. Why did that thought not fill me with hope and happiness? Why was it that the only thing I could think about at that pronouncement was never seeing his beautiful face again? Of never being touched again?

Although the change he'd hoped for hadn't come to pass, I'd grown accustomed to hands on my body, to warm, close cuddles, to kisses, to passion. I'd tasted the lips of another living being, and he had, in return, tasted mine. To go from that intimacy to the ocean seemed cold and wrong.

"You wouldn't keep me?" There was a small catch in my voice when I asked. I wondered if I might plead with him to keep me as a pet.

"If I can't make your body want mine, there seems no point. Why torture ourselves with this incompleteness? It would only breed resentment in both of us."

A tear trailed down the side of my face. I missed my family and the ocean, but I didn't want him to give up on me and toss me aside. Was that the only value I held for him? As some sexual toy? Could he not find something else to enjoy about me? But I knew I was being irrational. When you desire someone so much and you can't truly have them, everything else feels like a meaningless void.

He kissed the tears off my face and gave me another glass of wine. I drank it down to make the fuzzy feeling more pronounced, to feel warm when I was starting to grow cold.

His cock was hard and erect. Even thinking of that word for his anatomy felt so carnal. It was a carnality that a part of me had awakened to, but the rest still refused to accept could be part of my life.

This time, he shook his head when I tentatively moved to wrap my hand around him. "No. Use your mouth this time."

I'd known this was coming and was surprised he hadn't

demanded it sooner. Each day in his room, I'd expected him to take advantage of the one warm orifice he had access to. His self-control had only heightened my anxiety as the threat loomed larger.

Now his command started the twitch and flicker and flame. My heart beat faster. I *did* want him. I knew if enough time passed between us that eventually his pronouncement about seducing me, of winning, would come true.

But there was always the part of me I held back because I was trying to stay in both worlds at once. I knew that wasn't possible, and that I had to pick. Even though I was beginning to dread the cold fingers of the sea, imagining his warm, solid fingers in their place ... I still fought against closing the door of choice completely.

I closed my eyes and took him into my mouth. The new experience felt wicked, but it wasn't distasteful as I'd feared it might be. The memory of the couple having sex in the sand came unbidden, and I looked past the undignified nature of the act to see something that could be beautiful. A low moan came from my throat as I imagined limbs entangled and that look of surrender on her face.

The flame grew, and the memory morphed into a fantasy. Now it was me rolling in the sand with Kyros. He continued to stroke me as I licked and kissed and sucked. I felt myself let go and be in the moment. I surrendered, and for that brief minute or so I belonged completely to him. Not just physically stuck on land where I couldn't get back to my home, but in every cell of my being.

I didn't really feel what happened next. It wasn't painful. It should have been but it wasn't. Or maybe it was and I've just blocked it out now; I'm not sure. But what I remember was the sound. It was like thick cloth ripping. I jerked away and looked down.

It was happening; there would be no more swimming with my family. He'd held out the hope in front of me, and I'd relaxed, let my guard down. And now my body had decided for me. I watched in fascinated horror as the transformation took over, as my fin ripped down the middle and everything folded and reknitted, like clay being molded into a new design.

I shut my eyes because I couldn't watch my scales smooth into skin or the color change to match the top half of me. I buried my face in Kyros' chest as he held me and told me things were going to be okay. How were they going to be okay? They weren't ever going to be okay.

Several minutes passed before the change stopped. His hand cupped below the curvature of my waist, this new body part I had. It felt obscene, so wrongly intimate for him to touch a part of me that even I had never touched.

"Let's get you cleaned up," he said.

He helped me out of the bed and guided me on the walk to the bathroom. Walk. On land. I was moving on land. My new legs hurt. They were sore and achy, and I hoped that was just because they were new. If he'd let go of my waist, I would have fallen. I could barely propel myself forward as it was. The instinct was for everything below my waist to move as one unit swishing back and forth. This constant separation as one leg moved in front of the other was so disorienting, a wave of dizziness came over me.

"You'll get the hang of it," he said.

I'd expected to be put in a tub like before, but instead he took me over to a clear box and stood me up. Then water poured over me like rain. I cringed reflexively, waiting for something bad to happen as the freshwater flowed over me, but nothing. No salt. And yet things were fine.

Kyros braced my hands against the wall and then got in behind me, lathering me up with soap all over. I cried the whole time.

"Shhhh, Nerina," he soothed as he moved down to my waist and that new place between my thighs that throbbed every time his rough voice rumbled over me. This place felt like the new epicenter of me.

He spread my legs and looked at me with new fascination. His thumb stroked over what I instinctively knew was a private area. So weird to feel that way, after being indifferent about my own nudity for so long.

"I wonder if you'll grow hair here," he murmured, more to himself than to me.

Why would I grow hair there? Did women have hair there? Somehow that idea struck me as very vulgar. But then I'd heard that humans grew hair in odd places. Like under their arms and even on their legs. Merfolk didn't do that, so maybe I'd stay bare below my waist. I very much hoped so, not only because I didn't like the idea of hair but because I wanted there to still be something about me that made me the old Nerina. Something that felt like home.

A moment later his finger prodded at my opening, and then he was pushing it just inside my entrance. I gasped at the feeling, for a moment forgetting about everything I'd given up for this.

As soon as his finger was moving inside me, my brain started to catalog the new sensations. The twitch, the throb, the flicker, the flame. It was all part of a sexual symphony. I didn't know how the symphony played for a man, but I knew it built into something amazing, something I might be about to experience.

I finally understood why women were willing to debase themselves for this. I knew my mother would be absolutely horrified, but I didn't care. All I cared about was that Kyros didn't stop touching me. My legs hurt and were weak, still my hips arched reflexively toward him, moving in tandem with his fingers.

He sat in the clear box, his mouth on the bits of flesh I hadn't even gotten a good look at because they were so tucked away. And he was there, running his fingers along the folds of skin, followed swiftly by his tongue.

"Nerina, I'm going to fuck you, but first you're going to come for me."

I felt my face flame over this pronouncement. Never had he used the term *fuck* with me. It was so coarse, real. He'd been holding something back, something that had previously been too wild for me, that would have had me pulling away from him so that the transformation couldn't happen.

Now it occurred to me that with no ocean home to go back to, I was truly dependent on him. Without Kyros, where would I go? What would I eat? How would I survive? I felt desperate now to stay on his good side, which was strange because he'd never shown me his bad side, not really. He'd been so careful with me, and I wondered if that was about to change now that he had what he wanted.

As his tongue delved inside of me, devouring me like the appetizer I'd feared I'd become, my sexual innocence started to melt away. After all, how much innocence can one really claim with a man's tongue in her inner sanctum?

I gripped his shoulders for support. I felt like a jellyfish, my legs all spongy and unable to stand upright without assistance. He was too lost in me to notice.

I didn't understand at the time that he was playing with me, teasing me, drawing things out so that it would be better in the end. I thought this was the main event. Imagine my surprise when his tongue swirled over the spot where all the nerve endings came together.

Sounds started coming out of me that would never have come out of my mouth before: moans, gasps, groans, keening sounds. I wasn't sure if he was killing me or giving me pleasure. When my first orgasm finally swept over me, I thought I had died for a minute.

I rode the feeling as I would have ridden the back of a dolphin over the waves. I would never get tired of this or anything he did that would make these sensations happen. I felt like an addict, and I'd only had the first hit. I became lost for a moment thinking of what he could turn me into with this much pent-up desire in me. What would I do to feel this feeling?

Anything.

"My naughty little sea nymph," he whispered against my skin.

"I'm not a sea nymph anymore," I said, coming back to myself, remembering the awful finality of what I'd done, what I'd allowed myself to feel with him. I started crying again.

Kyros shut the water off and carried me back to the bedroom. He wrapped a towel around me and laid me on the bed. His pace was leisurely. He had all the time in the world now.

He was hard again, and I knew exactly where he wanted to put his cock. A sticky kind of wetness flowed out between my legs. I would have been disgusted by it, but Kyros seemed intrigued and pleased.

"Tell me you love me, Nerina."

I was taken aback by the request. Is this how it worked for humans? I'd always been intrigued by the concept of love. I'd heard about it, but it's not an emotion my kind can feel. We just aren't made that way. All of our emotions are more muted. More steady. We don't experience a lot of extremes, and love is an extreme.

But I'd been with this man long enough to know that all he wanted from me was my surrender, and although I didn't feel the feeling, I wanted to give him what would make him happy. So maybe it wasn't all a lie when the words passed through my lips.

"I love you, Master." The utterance tasted like dark chocolate on my tongue, warm, inviting. Sinful, decadent. Words I wished were truer. I'm not sure if he cared that they weren't true. He only wanted my obedience. He wanted to wring the words from my mouth every day until they hypnotized my mind into submission.

"Touch yourself," he said. "Rub your lovely little clit for me."

I played naïve for about five seconds, the time it took for him to take my hand and move it between my legs. There was an undeniable exercise of his rights over me in that moment as he watched me explore myself for the first time.

Probably other women have this moment privately. After all, they have years before they reach adulthood to discover what is what beneath their waist. Still, there was a part of me that was glad Kyros was there to watch. It was new and scary, and I didn't want to be alone.

My fingers skimmed along the folds of skin, finding the

new wetness strange and intriguing. I shuddered as I touched the little bit of skin Kyros had focused his attention on only minutes before under the water.

"Come again, Nerina."

I knew from the heat in my cheeks that they were red. I wasn't sure why. It had to be this new association of nudity with sex. Now I couldn't separate the two. I couldn't think of one without the other. There were no naked male or female forms in my head anymore that weren't fucking. Even merfolk, in my mind's eye, would now sinuously rub against one another, somehow replicating the pleasure my fingers were delivering at an increasing pace.

I spread my legs wider for no other reason than to give Kyros a better view. I don't know where that initiative came from. He smiled at me and the heat in my cheeks took flight and traveled down the length of my body. Then everything lit up and exploded. I arched off the bed, then dropped in a blissful heap, no doubt with a dopey grin on my face.

It was at this moment that Kyros chose to take me. I was floating in the feel-good haze, but not enough that it didn't hurt. It was a deep, sharp pain that made me recoil and try to scramble away from him, but he held tight, surging inside me hard and fast.

He smelled salty, like the sea, and I breathed him in like a substitute to try to soothe away the pain. But we weren't really together just now. He was in his head; I was in mine.

For a moment my mind went down a crazy track where I thought perhaps my humanity could have been reversed, perhaps my fin would have regrown if we hadn't breached this one, final territory.

While I hadn't felt my fin rip apart, this was different. *Two things lost in one night.* After several minutes, he let out a roar and stopped. I had to look into his eyes to determine if it was a good sound or a bad sound, to see if he was somehow displeased with me. But his face looked peaceful and contented.

At least one of us was peaceful and content. I didn't have another orgasm because my head wasn't in the right place for it. No one had told me that for a woman, losing one's virginity could feel like a trauma. I'd never been indoctrinated with any particular views of sex, except that it was some dirty thing animals did, and yet still, this felt like a bigger deal than I wanted it to be. And I hadn't even been there for it. Not really. I felt like it had happened, and except for the pain, I'd missed it.

For my own pleasure before, yes, I'd been there. But this new activity ... sex ... it felt more isolating than joining, and I worried it would always feel that way. I didn't say any of this to Kyros because I didn't know what he'd do with me if I couldn't enjoy the things humans enjoyed.

But he didn't demand a peek inside my head; he just held me cuddled against him while I cried.

"I'm sorry it hurt. I tried to be gentle. You felt so good wrapped around me." He stroked my hair, holding me close, and I didn't know what to feel. I only knew that something completely primal and final had been invoked between us. Something sealed in blood. As if to prove the point, I moved my hand between my legs. Just as I suspected. Red.

THAT NIGHT WAS THE FIRST NIGHT I DIDN'T SLEEP IN THE POOL. It wasn't just that I didn't, but that I couldn't. I couldn't breathe underwater anymore, and so I had to sleep in the bed with Kyros.

It was odd sleeping with someone else's skin pressed against mine, our limbs entangled. I could feel his erection pressed against me most of the night. It would be so easy for him to shift just slightly and be inside me, since we were both naked under the blankets. But he didn't.

Neither of us got much sleep that night, me because I was mourning the loss of the sea and the finality of what I'd allowed him to awaken in me, and Kyros because my crying kept him awake. But he didn't yell at me or hurt me or send me away to another room. I knew he could have done any of those things. His castle was large and surely had many rooms where he could stow me away until morning so he could sleep undisturbed by my anguish.

Maybe he was afraid I'd run away. But where would I run? I didn't even know how to run.

I had no clothing, and I was highly aware of that fact, as well as what the other men might try to do with me now that it would be so easy for them without the logistical quandary of a fish's fin. How would I care for myself? Where would I go? He had to know I would stay.

He stroked my back for so long I lost track of the time. He didn't say anything. What was there to say? I wondered if he regretted it, if he felt guilty for taking so much from me. But all he did was rub my back until I finally cried myself to sleep.

My dreams were of the sea. My family. The entire time I'd been with Kyros, I'd dreamed of him and the great temptation I'd succumbed to. And now I was dreaming of the sea. It seems we always want what we don't have or can't have, never what is right in front of us at the moment.

When I woke, Kyros was already dressed, and a cart had

been rolled in. There were two plates with meat and many fruits and a couple of flaky biscuits shaped like half of a moon. I sat in the chair that had been brought up to the cart and just stared at the plate and flatware.

I'd watched my Master using utensils, but he'd never fed me that way. When he'd fed me it had been straight from his hand. These smooth bits of silver with prongs were too impersonal, and I couldn't imagine eating that way.

"Nerina?"

I looked up at him, feeling the tears well in my eyes about to spill out again. I didn't say anything in reply. What was there to say? He didn't push the issue; he just got up from the table and went to the closet. He came out with a black silk robe.

"Come here," he said.

I couldn't walk on my own without his help, so I went down to my hands and knees. Crawling was easier. I looked up at him about halfway there and was taken aback by a dark hunger in his eyes, and somehow I realized that watching me crawl did something carnal to him.

When I reached him, I could see his erection tenting his pants. He gripped underneath my elbows and brought me to stand, then helped me into the robe. He tied it around my waist, and I tried to memorize the way he did it with the loops and wrapping the belt around them, then pulling it tight into a bow. In the sea we didn't have anything we tied like that.

"Go to the pool, I'll be right behind you."

"I ... " Did he expect me to crawl? What about the stairs? I reasoned that I'd slithered on my belly to get down a set of stairs the first night when I'd still had my fin, but that was different. I lived here now.

"Crawl." he said.

He'd been holding on to my waist, steadying me after he'd tied the robe shut. Now he let go and stepped out of my reach. I went immediately to my knees, too unsteady to stand and walk without assistance. I imagined with a wall nearby I could have started learning to walk, but at the moment, a wall was too far away and the fierce look in Kyros' eyes stopped those thoughts in their tracks.

Obediently I turned and started to crawl from the room. I heard a sound catch in his throat, and I knew this turned him on, and that whether I could walk or not, he'd ask me to do this again. The slow, answering throb between my legs made clear that he wasn't the only one who found this somehow erotic. I tensed, wondering if he'd lose all control and fling the robe up over my back to kneel behind and take me.

I didn't know how I felt about that. Despite not having an orgasm during sex, there was an odd sort of comfort in being possessed by someone.

I could hear his footsteps behind me as I made my way downstairs. I let my arms do most of the work on the descent, much as I had that first night. When I got to the room with the pool, I crawled to the edge and waited, my body humming as I sensed his approach. He shut the door softly and brought the plates over to the edge.

"Get in and swim."

I stared at the pool for a good minute. I'd been mourning the loss of the sea and now that I was looking at a piece of it, being allowed to swim in it, I didn't know what to do. With a fin and no ability to drown, it had been natural. Now I wasn't sure.

"I don't think I know how."

He raised an eyebrow at me. "You've swam your whole life, and you've watched me. Get in and try."

"I ... can't even stand well." As a mermaid the idea of not being able to stand in the water, of even standing at all, had been so foreign it had been laughable, but now I was desperate for my legs to work because I needed them to support me.

"Nerina. Do as I say. I won't let anything bad happen to you."

The look in his eyes was so fiercely protective that I became more afraid of disappointing him than of the water. I eased myself in and gripped the side of the pool for balance. I could stand in this depth but still feared falling and going under. I was torn between crying and laughing over the absurdity. Me, afraid of water.

"You've watched me swim every morning. You know what to do," he said, his legs now in the pool, brushing against my hip.

"What if I can't? What if I go under?"

"Then I'll come get you."

I knew he would, but even so, I didn't want to risk it.

The door opened and a servant walked in. Her eyes widened when she saw me in the pool, obviously with legs now. Or perhaps it was my nudity that startled her. Like Estella, the woman who had brought linens, this woman, though younger, seemed equally prim and proper. She held two glasses of juice, sat them beside the plates, then averted her eyes from me and left.

I can't recall how I moved my arms or how I breathed or held my breath, or how I kicked out. I just did it. I didn't think. It was as natural as it had been in the ocean, which made me feel silly for worrying about it. The water was my true home and always would be. Legs or no legs.

Even so, the salt water wasn't a necessity for life. We were now two separate things, Nerina and the water. Where before we had been one, blending and merging together until I could never tell where I ended and the sea began. Once I got past this new sensation, I got used to the way my legs sliced through the water, so different from how I'd moved with a fin, but no less enjoyable.

Finally I swam back to Kyros. When I gripped the edge of the pool for support, he pressed a strawberry into my mouth. For the first time since I'd lost my fin, I smiled.

I assumed after breakfast that he'd go off and leave me for a while. Maybe in the pool, or maybe in the bedroom. Surely he had other business to attend to besides seducing me. But instead he left the plates and glasses behind for the servants to clean up and ordered me out of the water. When it proved impossible under my own steam and I started to panic, he lifted me out, then wrapped a towel around me and led me to the stairs.

"What about the robe?" I asked. It still was crumpled on the stone floor next to our abandoned meal.

"Leave it. You won't be needing it."

This made me apprehensive. I was well aware of what he intended to do with me if I wouldn't be needing the robe. I still wasn't sure if I really *liked* sex. I liked all the things that had led up to it, and the pleasure he'd produced in me, but sex itself had hurt and I was afraid it would continue to hurt every time we did it.

This time he helped me walk. It was slow going, but he was patient. I watched my feet the whole time. For the first time since the transformation I was able to bring myself to look at them. Really look at them. They were a marvel of bio-mechanics. I'd always thought my fin was special, but I couldn't comprehend the number of bones and muscles that must make up the human foot. Maybe I could learn to appreciate my new legs and feet. There were so many new things I could learn to do. Walk, run, climb, dance. Then my mind started to go down less pure paths, imagining all the different positions Kyros could get me into now that I had legs.

When we got back to his room, he looked me over, assessing. "Are you cold?"

"No, Master." I blushed because while I was aware of the faint trembling that had started in my limbs, I'd thought I'd successfully kept it concealed from him. Now, my first full day as a human, I was even more afraid than I'd been back when I could be put on the dinner menu.

After several days with him, I'd convinced myself I wouldn't become human and he might not kill me. I'd go back to the sea eventually, so the idea that being with Kyros was going to be a long-term situation hadn't really entered my mind. When events had played out in my head, it was always a few weeks at most. Either I'd be killed or released when he got bored with hoping I'd change into something that could never be.

But now that it had happened, it was finally sinking in just how permanent my living arrangements were. I was keenly aware as his erection pressed against my skin, that he had every intention—and in his mind, every right—to use me for his own pleasure as often as he wanted.

Since having breakfast in the pool, I still held out a hope that he wasn't going to turn vicious now that he had what he wanted: access. But that still didn't mean I'd like all the things he did to me.

He finally spoke again. "Are you afraid of me, sea nymph?"

I couldn't be sure whether or not he was mocking me with

the endearment. I didn't answer the question because I wasn't sure what the answer was. I was afraid, I just wasn't sure if it was him or something more nebulous and hard to pin down.

Instead I said, "I miss my family. I'll never see them again." It wasn't the answer to his question, but it weighed on me considerably.

His grip on me tightened and for a moment I thought he intended to squeeze me to death. After a minute or two, he seemed to realize what he was doing and loosened his hold.

His mouth was next to my ear, the warm puffs of his breath on my skin sending another shiver through me. "I'm going to make you forget them." Lips grazed my throat and then across my shoulders as his hands moved to cup my breasts. I sagged against him, rendered unable to stand by the electricity in his touch.

"Tell me you love me, Nerina."

"I love you, Master." It still wasn't true. I wasn't sure if it ever could be. And yet the idea to disobey a direct order wouldn't even form in my brain. He had the power to turn me from an innocent mermaid into a sexual animal. What other powers might he possess?

His fingers stroked down my belly, moving between my thighs to part moist folds of flesh. Moisture that wasn't from the pool.

After a long stretch of silence, he said, "I'll inform your family that you're all right."

It wasn't unheard of for humans to try to communicate with mermaids. They often dropped smooth large stones in the sea with messages, or sometimes put messages in bottles that were weighted down so they would go beneath the water.

A legend of my people is that merfolk were so curious

about the messages dropped into the ocean that they learned how to read and decipher their meaning.

We'd find these messages and laugh over them. Often they were of a sexual nature, which both fascinated and disgusted us. If Kyros sent several messages about where I was, would someone from my family find it? Would they believe him?

"What will you say?"

"That you're human now and living with me in the castle on the hill, and that if they want to come see you, they will not be harmed or held against their will."

"They won't believe you." We aren't a very trusting sort. In all likelihood, even if they found the message, they would think it was some sort of trap. Mermaid fin *was* a delicacy, after all.

I felt him shrug against me, and it seemed the matter was closed for now. He was more interested in other activities. I gasped as he scooped me up and took me to the bed. My breath caught in my throat and I moved away from him. I'm not sure what I thought I was accomplishing, trying to edge away from him so that he wouldn't notice what I was doing. It was more an instinct to avoid pain than anything else.

"I'm not going to hurt you," he soothed as he brushed my hair from my face.

"It hurt last night."

"I know. But that was just the first time. It won't hurt today."

I wasn't sure if I believed him, but I didn't have much choice in the matter.

"Spread your legs."

I was still very self-conscious, but I did what he asked because his voice and hands were still so gentle that I felt if I just obeyed him, I could prolong the kindness indefinitely. He stroked me for awhile, and finally he spoke again.

"I need you to relax."

"I'm not sure I can."

He gave me an exasperated look. In the sea I'd been independent and strong-willed, but taken out of my element and put in this frightening new environment, I'd lost all my fight. I couldn't be blamed in the beginning because I'd had a fin and a huge disadvantage.

But now I walked ... sort of. I at least had crawling down. And yet, the idea of escape hadn't spent more than a couple of minutes in my mind. Mermaids don't do well alone. We need to be surrounded by others. My kind was now forever separated from me and being a part of Kyros' family was the only option left. My instincts turned to pleasing him so I wouldn't be alone.

I was perhaps as exasperated with myself and my sudden refrains of *can't* as my Master, but I wasn't sure how to fix the situation. While I pondered all this, Kyros settled between my legs, his wet tongue darting out to lick me.

I shuddered the moment his tongue made contact with the sensitive flesh. The discomfort in being touched from earlier in my captivity was a dim memory now as every nerve ending awakened and fired to life with each human touch.

It was said that mermaids had hypnotic magic that lured sailors to their deaths, but in reality, we sometimes liked to sun ourselves on rocks that were safe because of how hard it would be for a human to reach us. It wasn't our fault the men liked to look and often wrecked their boats and died.

No, the real hypnotic powers rested with humans. With the way they could touch you and make you forget you didn't like to be touched. How they could create a type of alchemy in a mermaid's body chemistry that made her want more and then somehow made that *more* possible.

The intensity of the strokes of his tongue were unrelenting as my hips bucked against his mouth. His hands gripped underneath me, hard, pulling me to him. I was sure there would be fingerprints left where he dug into my cheeks. A few minutes later, that now familiar feeling happened, like a flower bud opening.

"That's it, Nerina, come for me."

The deep purr of his voice as it vibrated against my clit sent another wave of pleasure over me. A moment later and he was inside me, his cock straining against my walls. It was still a tight fit, but he was right, it didn't hurt this time.

I closed my eyes against his intense stare. It was too intimate. I was afraid for a moment that he'd make me open them. Maybe it wasn't enough for him to dominate and control my body, maybe he needed my soul, too. But he allowed me my privacy and didn't intrude.

Twitch.

My eyes shot open at the sensation. It was a little different than what I'd felt when I'd had a fin. The hint that something was about to happen and change remained the same. This time it came from deeper inside, and yet, it was there. Then the feeling went away and he came inside me.

I thought we were done, but we were far from it. His fingers went back to stroking between my legs.

"Every time I let you come, I want you to beg me for more. I'll determine when you've had enough. Do you understand?"

"Yes, Master."

For a moment, fear cramped my stomach. What he implied was too intense for me. Even with the changes that had happened, I couldn't imagine having that feeling happen over and over, no matter how pleasurable it was. It seemed like too much of a good thing, like getting sick on too much rich or sweet food.

Time lost meaning as I lost track of the orgasms. My ability to count them failed me past ten; of course I could count higher than that under normal circumstances. There was an odd sort of conflict raging inside me. A part of me wished he would stop this torture. But every time I wished that, my body would recover from the last bout of pleasure and surge upward toward another wave, greedily reaching for more. By the time he was finished, I was wrung out, the sweat a fine sheen on my body, making me glisten in an almost iridescent way.

"Nerina?" he prompted after my last orgasm.

"Please Master, may I have more?" I prayed silently that he would end it so I could rest. He'd only fucked me the one time so I couldn't imagine what he was getting out of this beyond the thrill of the power of manipulating my body, playing it like his instrument, figuring out which touches would make me create which sounds. Perhaps he was writing his own music.

"No, I think you've had enough," he said.

I sighed, and I'm sure the relief was evident on my face. He chuckled and then mounted me again. I don't know if it was because I'd been so wet and aroused, or because I was so sensitive from so many orgasms, but as his cock pushed deep inside me, the twitch turned into a full and growing flame.

His smug smile made it clear that he'd seen the change on my features. Something was building, something new and more terrifying than the other orgasms I'd already grown accustomed to. As he pounded harder, something inside me opened up and let go. It was like an endless fall.

I grabbed on to his shoulders, burying my face in his neck, clinging to him. I felt warm, hot, tingly. This time the pleasure came from deep inside, so strong it was almost an ache. I felt my hips thrusting in tandem with his, trying to take him deeper still, trying to crawl inside of him until the feeling exploded. I was sure if his arms hadn't been wrapped around me that I would have literally come apart.

"Now we're done," he said as I shook against him. "You can go take a bath if you like."

When he moved off me I attempted to get off the bed and my legs immediately turned to jelly. I caught myself on the floor with my hands. I couldn't walk yet unaided under the best circumstances, and even crawling was proving difficult at the moment.

Kyros laughed, a deep, rumbling chuckle that was more garden-variety mirth than mockery.

I shot him a dirty look, but he'd already closed his eyes and lain back on the bed. I did want to sit in water. Even if it wasn't salt water, it was centering somehow. I crawled to the bathroom and turned the faucet on. Living in the sea had given me a tolerance and preference for cooler water, so I kept it cooler in what I now privately thought of as the rain box.

That night I slept more easily. The silky sheets whispering across my legs were almost equivalent to the comfort of the water I'd slept submerged under before the change. My dreams were muted, a series of images that never seemed to crystallize into a storyline. The lack of anything solid to hold on to in my nocturnal adventures made me feel unsteady somehow. As the wispy tendrils of images receded, I reached out for the comfort of Kyros' body, wanting to cling to him in my first moments of wakefulness because he was solid. Real.

But he wasn't there. There was a note on his pillow for me saying he'd been called away to take care of some business and he'd return in a few hours. A toga was draped across the bed with a golden sash. The breakfast cart was rolled next to the bed. I couldn't believe I'd managed to sleep through all this activity around me, especially when my sleep hadn't felt very deep.

I hated eating alone, hated not eating in the pool with him feeding me, but I slipped the fabric over my head and ate anyway. I caught my image in a reflecting glass and smiled. I looked very much like the images of Greek goddesses in the paintings on the walls that my Master seemed to admire so much. I felt a warmth in my stomach that he would pick something for me to wear that made me look like his paintings.

I lifted the silver tray from the cart to find eggs, fruit, and the half-moon shaped bread I was coming to love. There was a glass of milk instead of juice this morning. I'd never had milk. Well, besides mermaid milk when I was a baby, which I don't remember. This, I was sure, didn't come from a mermaid or a human. I decided I was a fan of this beverage and would ask Kyros if I could have it more often in the future.

After I ate, I decided to practice walking. First I sat on the bed, just moving my legs, flexing my feet, wiggling my toes. I grabbed on to the stone wall, using the crevices for a better grip, to help steady myself. My balance was woefully wobbly, and I feared I'd never be able to walk like a normal person, but as I moved, watching my feet and how they reacted to the ground underneath me, I slowly became more confident. Not confident enough to let go of the wall, but confident enough that I almost felt like I was moving normally.

I was still a little sore and weak, but my lower limbs were getting used to movement and becoming surer of their increasing abilities.

I tried the door. It wasn't locked. I don't know if I expected it to be. In his note, he hadn't given me any orders about staying in his room, so I used the opportunity to explore.

The castle was enormous and fairly dark in the hallways. I almost felt as if I needed some kind of fire or electricity to find my way. Thankfully a few doors were open that led to other rooms, allowing the sunlight from their windows to spill out into the hallway, creating small patches of brightness to light my way.

As I walked, I tried to take a few steps here and there without touching the wall. After a couple of hours of wandering and practicing, I was walking without much pain and without need of the wall for balance. Whatever magic had made my legs had made them fully functional and properly muscled. Nothing had come to me atrophied or in disrepair. I simply had to get oriented and used to moving in this way.

At the end of one hall was a set of spiraling stairs that went up into a tower. This new challenge was almost enough to make me turn around. I wasn't sure if I could walk up stairs, especially so many. But the steps were solid and stone, with walls on both sides and a rail to steady myself. It would be great practice.

The tower was many stories high and quite a struggle to climb, but I made it to the top. I gaped at my surroundings when I reached the tower. What I'd always believed about the nature of Anostos was untrue.

While Anostos is characterized by hazy red clouds with no real determinable night or day, what happened high above those clouds many stories up was a different matter. The large room at the top of the tower was little more than a domed glass window. A section of it opened, allowing something on a tripod to nestle there. The object had a lens on both ends. I wasn't sure what the nature of this object was, but it seemed to have something to do with exploring the sky.

I laughed. I could look at the sun and the moon and the stars again. It was another of the things I'd thought I'd lost forever when I lost the sea. I could imagine Kyros and I laying on mats and blankets up here under the stars. Someday I would work up the courage to ask if we could.

The sun shone on me, and I wanted to live in this room. It brought back memories of sunning myself on rocks in other parts of Meropis. I stood in the warmth of the sun for a long time, then finally made my way back down the stairs.

When I reached the floor with all the bedrooms on it, I checked Kyros' room to make sure he hadn't returned. I didn't want him angry with me for being gone, but I was excited to show him my progress.

There was no evidence that he'd come back from his business, but the tray and scraps of leftover food had been removed. Perhaps by Estella. Or maybe by the woman I'd seen the other day at the pool. Maybe someone else entirely.

I went back out into the dark hallway and was faced with two choices. One was a large, curved stone staircase that would likely open out into some main entry hall, and the other was the back set of stairs that I'd gone down the first night during the party. The back stairs would open out near the kitchen, which I was sure would be occupied by servants.

I wasn't sure which set of stairs would be better to avoid running into someone. The quietness of the castle after the food's removal indicate that no one was frantically looking for me. Surely everyone here must be aware of my presence and who I was. Maybe that was what bothered me the most, the idea that if they saw me with my new legs, they would know how I'd gotten them—they probably already knew. The change marked me in a way that was more exposing than my kind was accustomed to.

Finally I decided on the main staircase. If this was going to be my home, I wasn't going to hide in it like some mouse. My bare feet made no sound over the cool stone steps as I descended, holding on to the railing for support.

The main entry hall was empty, but I could hear a soft din of female voices in the distance, I assumed the kitchen. I moved away from the voices and discovered the room with the pool that had served as my room, and then a ballroom, and a library, and a few other rooms whose purposes I wasn't exactly sure of. On the main level toward the back of the castle was another set of stairs that went down.

Much like the tower had, these spiraled, but there were fewer steps. Downstairs was even darker than the hallways. I felt along the wall for a source of light and found a switch. The switch didn't make it much better. It certainly didn't make it bright. Hundreds of smallish wall lights illuminated all at once, enough to see what was down there, but not enough to read by.

Strange contraption after strange contraption filled my vision. I couldn't begin to guess what all of these things were for, but they seemed in some way meant for humans. They seemed like torture devices of some sort. The kinds of things mermen liked to tell stories about to scare the rest of us.

Hanging from the walls were long strips of leather and other things I didn't have names for but that equally scared me. After the hours of practicing and going up and down so many steps, I'd become accustomed to my legs enough that I could walk across the stone floor without aide of the wall. I occasionally and reluctantly touched one of the free-standing contraptions in the room to help steady myself on the few times my balance failed me.

It was all very puzzling, yet also sinister. I wasn't sure what any of this was for, but it seemed it couldn't be for good. If this was my master's castle, then he must be aware of this room, perhaps even used it. That thought, along with the cool dampness in the room, sent a shiver down my spine.

"I thought I saw someone come down here."

I turned quickly, recognizing the voice. Male. Not my Master. Aric. The fisherman who had shown too much interest in me the day they'd brought me to Kyros' chambers. He smiled, not a friendly smile. He smelled of fish from the sea, and something else I couldn't name. The odor was so pungent it reached me from across the room.

The smell made me want to vomit. At first I thought I wanted my family, but in my mind my mother's arms wrapped around me and held me close. That wasn't the way of my kind. No, what I wanted right now, the type of comfort I sought, I could only get from a human.

For the first time, I didn't long for my fin or the sea. My fin might have protected me more from the lecherous fisherman, but the only thing I wanted was for Kyros to be with me, his arms wrapped tightly around me.

Aric stepped closer. "Pretty mermaid. I see you just became a more convenient conquest." His eyes traveled the length of my body and I could almost see the images bloom in his mind. I could guess what they were. He didn't seem to be much of a thinker, so they probably weren't imaginative images, but instead primal, simple: my legs spread with him inside me. I shuddered and backed away, putting one of the scary contraptions between us.

"Come now, don't be that way," he said, his approach not slowing. If I could somehow move as fast as the beating of my heart, I could get away from those measured thundering steps of his, but I found myself rooted to the spot.

I still hadn't managed to form a word. Perhaps if I screamed someone would come help me. I opened my mouth to do it, but quickly closed it again. What if they wanted what the fisherman wanted? Or worse? What if they wanted to watch? I wished I had the kind of mental magic sailors accused us of. I wished I could make Aric drop dead, or that I could will my Master to the scene.

"I bet I'm more gentle than the Master. He's got dark tastes, as I'm sure you're aware. Does he bring you down here often?"

The question caught me so off guard that my vocal chords spontaneously reactivated. "W-what?"

"Oh, don't play coy with me. I know he must have whipped that pretty little ass I'm sure you've got hidden away. He should keep you naked, the way you came to us from the sea." He reached me then, his hand curled like a claw as he gripped the fabric, ripping it away from my flesh until my breasts were bared to his gaze.

I struggled to cover myself, my modesty around strangers having risen to ridiculous proportions because now I knew too much about the pleasures humans fed from.

"Gotten all prissy on us have you? You weren't so good when you came out of the ocean. You could have been an appetizer, don't forget. Must be a great cocksucker for him to have let you live."

He reached down to start undoing his pants. I could feel

the tears streaming down my face and something inside me yelled *Run!* I didn't know how to run. I could barely walk and climb stairs, but the voice in my head sounded like Kyros, and so I obeyed. I didn't think, I just moved, just like in the water when he'd told me to swim.

As Aric stumbled in his half-removed pants, it occurred to me what the other smell was. He was drunk. I gained confidence as I started to notice his own slight unsteadiness made greater with his pants no longer around his waist.

I raced up the stairs, stumbling a couple of times, not looking back. My legs burned from the exertion I wasn't yet used to, but I didn't care. I ran straight for the kitchen because that was where I'd heard women's voices. They may not approve of me, but I hoped they didn't actively wish me ill.

I was panting when I reached the doorway and several women looked up, their mouths gaping open. I looked down to find my breasts still exposed. Blushing, I gathered the fabric to cover myself.

"What on earth?" Estella said.

"A-Aric," was all I could manage to get out.

"Did he?"

I knew what she was asking. These women seemed unable to express a full graphic sexual thought, but somehow a female language older than time took over. We all knew what we were talking about, even though we weren't really talking about it.

"He tried. Downstairs."

Estella and one of the other women exchanged a look that let me know they knew about the frightening things down below. The kitchen became a flurry of activity as the older woman guided me to a wooden table and started shouting orders. The others scurried off to follow her bidding.

One woman returned a few moments later with a blanket to wrap around me. Another put a bowl in front of me with soup she'd just ladled from a big pot on the stove. Another gave me some water and a generous chunk of fresh-baked bread.

It had been a while since breakfast, but since my fear had abated, the hunger response was even greater than it should have been. I'd had a similar situation once when I'd had to outswim a hungry shark.

Although Estella had shown disdain for me before, neither she nor any other woman in the kitchen showed it now. What had almost happened to me served as some sort of bond between us. We were united against a common foe: a man.

"Don't you worry," she said, patting my hand. The gesture caught me off-balance, as Kyros had been the only human flesh against my own until now. Aside from when the fishermen had brought me up to his room, of course. "When the Master gets home, he'll take care of everything."

I hoped that was true, yet Aric's words about my Master's darker urges, whatever those might be, lurked on the edges of my mind, making me almost fear seeing Kyros again. I hadn't been human long, and the possibilities of what he might yet do with me hadn't sunk in. At least not until I'd seen what was hidden beneath the castle.

A few moments later, Aric arrived, his pants still halfway about his legs, his ruddy little cock at full, unimpressive mast protruding obscenely toward us. There was a bottle in his hand.

"Wine just arrived!" he shouted, swinging the bottle out and sloshing some of its dark red contents out onto the floor. It made me think of blood and violence, and I shrank back farther from him, holding the blanket tight around me.

His eyes seemed to zero in on my movement like a shark and for a minute we were the only ones in the room. "Pretty little mermaid. Why did you run? I wanted to play. I had good games for us. I'm sure the Master will be happy to share his whore." Tears gathered in my eyes because I was cornered with nowhere to go.

It was at that moment that Estella started beating him on the head with a big wooden spoon. Of course. I wasn't alone this time. Panic made me forget.

"Ow, woman!"

The violence sobered him enough to pull his pants back up and fasten them. Estella's glare was fierce and protective, and I didn't feel so alone and hated here. The other kitchen staff armed themselves with utensils and cookware and stood in front of me.

"Crazy whores, the lot of you!" Aric said, sloshing more wine onto the floor. "I only came to share the happy news that the wine was here and finish business with the mermaid."

I realized now why it had taken me so long to realize he was drunk. He didn't slur his words. Who knew how long he'd been drinking or how much he'd had. He seemed able to hold his liquor more than most.

It was at that moment that Kyros showed up.

At first I didn't know what had happened. The room went deathly quiet and still. Then I peered around the hip of the woman standing directly in front of me.

Kyros took the bottle of wine from the fisherman's hand and smashed it against the wall. Everyone, including me, jumped.

"Someone had better explain what is going on this instant." I'd never heard his voice so sharp. He stood taller than Aric, broader, and far more imposing. And if not for the words still spinning in my brain about his desires, I might have been relieved to see him. Now I wasn't sure what to feel.

The kitchen workers were all clustered in a group, blocking me from his view. He moved them aside one by one until there was no obstruction between us.

"Nerina?"

"Yes, Master?" I'd been the victim, but I was so afraid he was going to hurt me. His loud voice and the smashing of the wine bottle as well as my uncertainty over whether I was even allowed to roam his house without permission had a tight knot forming in my stomach. I cringed away from him.

He looked around at the others in the room. "What's happened here?"

When the others remained silent, he took the blanket off me, as if it was necessary to prove his suspicion. His eyes darkened and narrowed. He was staring at me when he bellowed, "Aric!"

I closed my eyes against him. His anger didn't seem directed at me, at least not for the moment, still I couldn't look in his eyes when they were so dark. The fact that they could get like that at all was more than I could presently cope with. Feeling his stare on me, I grabbed the fabric of my clothing and held it together because it made me feel ashamed for Kyros to know what had almost happened downstairs.

On some level I knew it wasn't my fault, on another, I'd been somewhere I wasn't supposed to be, so it was easy to blame myself. I was afraid that once Kyros extracted the truth from me—and I knew he would—that he too would lay the blame at my feet, and then that malevolent gaze would be directed at me.

My breath came more shallowly, and I hunched my shoulders, my whole body turning in on itself like a turtle going into his shell. I wasn't able to relax and open my eyes until I heard his footsteps move away from me.

He gripped the fisherman by his collar and raised him off the ground. "What. Did. You. Do?" He practically hissed when he spoke.

"She asked for it. She begged me for it."

For one insane moment I feared Kyros would believe him. After all, they all knew the legends of mermaids and their supposed seductive powers, luring men to their deaths. There was real reason to fear my Master could be taken by such a lie.

Kyros set the man down on his feet then hauled back and punched him. Aric stumbled a bit and grabbed for the wall to hold himself upright. He laughed.

"You will stay the hell away from Nerina. Am I being clear?"

"You've shared other sluts you've bedded. Why not this one? She used her magic on me. She'll use it again. You can't trust the sea witch. I won't be held responsible for what I do next time I see her unattended." Aric's gaze shifted to me, showing me the full lewdness of his intent at our next encounter.

Kyros let out a guttural shout that sounded like some sort of war cry. His large hands reached out, gripped Aric's head firmly, and wrenched and twisted. The crack was so loud it filled the whole space of the kitchen. It had been too fast for the fisherman to react, and he slumped to the floor, dead.

My Master still stared at the fisherman as if he might

somehow magically reknit bone and get up. "Estella," Kyros said without taking his eyes off the corpse, "that's been a long time coming for him. Get rid of the body."

Then he turned back to me and everything inside me screamed to run. He seemed electrified, taken with an intense blood lust, not even seeing me properly, his rage was so great. Was that rage now directed at me? Did he believe the *sea witch* garbage?

"Master, please, I didn't … "

"Don't speak, Nerina."

I shut my mouth as he advanced. Estella and the kitchen staff were already acting on the Master's orders. Estella, being the substantial woman that she was, moved behind Aric's body and hefted him up, gripping under his arms. Two other women helped, each picking up one of his legs. Then they made their way down the hall.

I shuddered, thinking that perhaps they'd had to dispose of a body at a previous point in their work history, so coordinated was their action. As if they knew exactly where to go and what to do. No one was standing in front of me and guarding me now, although I desperately wished for that protection. Even if Aric had still been alive, he now felt like the least of my problems.

I was surprised when Kyros hauled me up to stand. His grip wasn't nearly as harsh as the anger that still radiated from his features. It was as if he were intentionally being gentler, controlling the force with which he touched me. I hoped that was a good sign as he led me out of the kitchen and down the hallway away from Estella and the other women.

Even as I was trying to convince myself he wasn't upset with me, my fear mounted. When we reached the main hall, my anxiety had reached its peak. I could still feel the anger coming off him. Seeing and hearing his violence and rage acted out against another made me fear what would become of me if I stayed with him. Aric's words about my Master's darker urges and his insinuation that Kyros had tortured women downstairs was the final deciding factor.

His grip on me was still gentle, gentle enough to break free. So I pulled away and bolted for the door.

Once outside the castle, I ran down the grassy hill, disoriented for a moment by the hazy red clouds all around me. They were thicker than normal and it made navigating more difficult as I could only see a few feet in front of me. But I could smell the sea, and my instincts told me which way to go to get home. I fell a couple of times. Running was still so new, but my need to get away from the castle aided me.

I knew I couldn't live in the sea anymore. I knew I couldn't survive out there, but I couldn't survive here either, and I was sure what lie waiting for me in the ocean would be quicker and less traumatic than whatever my Master's plans for me.

My greatest fear was not being able to get there in time, but with the haze of clouds, Kyros wouldn't be able to move overly fast, either. And he might not be able to find the water as quickly by instinct alone.

As my feet hit the beach and I got closer to the water, the haze started to clear enough so that I could see much farther ahead of me. I could see the waves now lapping the shore. Home. I didn't even care that the sea would ultimately kill me. I just wanted to end it and escape the human's wrath. Even if he wasn't angry with me, if what Aric said was true, and hadn't just been meant to scare me, then eventually Kyros would hurt me. And somehow I knew he'd drag it out a long time.

I didn't want to think he'd do something like that after the kindness and patience he'd shown me, but after watching him kill a man in front of me, I could no longer sugarcoat his ferocity.

The fishermen were all down the beach, quite some distance from me, so I felt safe to take the toga off.

The water was comforting as I stepped into it. I looked behind me to see Kyros getting closer. He didn't run, just walked at a steady pace as if he had all the time in the world. He must have thought I was trapped with nowhere to go and that he could therefore take his time.

"Nerina!"

I turned away from his voice and dove into the water. I would swim until I couldn't go any further and then I would let the sea take me under, back to my family where I belonged. As the water rushed around my moving form, I started to think that perhaps I could swim far enough before tiring to make it. Maybe I could swim around to another side of Meropis and escape him that way. The idea of being alone in another foreign place, with nothing but more human threats to look forward to, was equally unpleasant. No, it was better to just go home.

I'd gotten maybe a mile out when I could hear him gaining on me, another frantic disturbance in the water. When his arms finally wrapped around me, I struggled, kicking out at him.

"You'll take us both down. Stop it!" he shouted, his voice just as hard-edged and angry as it had been in the kitchen.

"Good! Go away. Leave me alone."

His arm went around my neck, pressing, tightening. I struggled harder but then everything went dark.

I was surprised to wake up in Kyros' bedroom, and at first

I thought it was a final dream before death. I'd thought his intent was to kill me, as if he couldn't give the sea that one victory; it had to be him. But he'd only meant to render me unconscious so I wouldn't fight him as he took us both back to the shore.

I found myself wrapped in a towel, a sudden chill sweeping over me.

"Here, drink this." He held out a mug of something hot and dark-colored, with steam rising off it. Some type of tea.

I took it, half-afraid it was poisoned, but then the logical side of my brain kicked in. If he'd wanted to kill me he could have just done it out in the ocean. There was no need to go to the trouble of bringing me back. And with the violence I knew he was capable of, there was no point in more civilized forms of murder.

As I drank the warm liquid, he reached out to brush the damp hair off my face with his fingertips. I jerked back, and he sighed.

"I'm not going to hurt you. You've done nothing wrong."

I'd done everything wrong, and we both knew it. I'd wandered all over his castle and gone somewhere I'd known I shouldn't. I'd run from him, fought him. I didn't believe it when he said I'd done nothing wrong and he wasn't going to hurt me. I just couldn't figure out why he was playing it this way. What was the benefit to him?

"Why did you run from me?"

I took another sip of the tea, trying to put off answering as long as possible. When the look on his face reached maximum impatience, I set the cup on the table beside the bed. "You killed a man, and you were still angry when you turned back to me. I was afraid."

"I was upset someone almost hurt you. It wasn't directed at you."

"That wasn't how it felt. Besides, it's enough that you showed that kind of anger to anyone. It means you have it inside you. How can I ever feel safe knowing that's coiled and waiting to strike?" Mermen weren't like that. They weren't angry or violent to anyone. We were a peaceful race. The scene in the kitchen and in the dungeon before only confirmed that I was now among barbarians and could never feel safe again.

He nodded and watched me for another minute. The formality between us had been abandoned for the moment in light of the morning's happenings.

"I would never harm you, Nerina. You have to know that by now. What's really going on?"

I could have explained the nature of my people to him, but it would have fallen on deaf ears. Besides, he was right. It wasn't really all about what happened in the kitchen. He'd killed a man, but he'd also removed a threat from me. I looked down at the floor, unable to meet his intense stare.

"I saw what's downstairs."

I expected anger, then pain, but it didn't come. Instead, he merely said, "I see," his voice mild and noncommittal. "And what did you think about what you saw in the dungeon?"

Dungeon. I didn't like the word, but it seemed to fit the dark, damp place. The contraptions, the cages, the strips of leather I somehow knew were meant to hurt people, and I couldn't understand why. I'd thought perhaps they were for dangerous enemies until Aric had filled my mind with a far worse scenario.

"Aric said you had dark desires and wondered if you took me down there a lot. Did you intend to take me down there?"

I chanced a look up at his face, desperately hoping to find some kindness in his eyes.

The kindness was there, but it didn't go with his answer. "Yes. And I still do."

I shook my head furiously. "No! Please."

"Yes." He moved closer to me and a panic filled my chest because I couldn't get up and away from him quickly enough, and anyway I knew he was faster than me and stronger than me, even with my new legs. I couldn't get away from whatever he intended to do, because I knew this time he wouldn't be foolish enough to loosen his grip.

I whimpered as his hand cupped my cheek. "Why didn't you just let me die in the sea? Are you going to hurt me because of what Aric said about me? I'm not a witch. I don't have any special powers."

"I know that. It's not because of Aric."

"Then why?" I'd thought I'd managed to find some reference point to understand humans and their strange ways, but this was beyond what I was capable of processing. There had to be something very wrong with him. It made the prospect of never getting away more dangerous than I'd ever feared.

"Nerina, there are many different types of pleasure. Some types look like pain to the untrained eye. I'll show you."

I couldn't accept what he was telling me, what he was implying that he intended to do with me. I thought perhaps it would just be a matter of discussion for now, that I'd still have time to talk him out of it since I'd just been dragged out of the sea unconscious. But he had other plans. Before I could react, he picked me up, still wrapped in the towel, and carried me down the main steps.

"No, please, Master. You can't. Please. I'll be good. I won't ever disobey you again."

"It's not about obedience or disobedience. I'm not going to punish you for anything that happened today. You were the victim, and you were scared. I understand that. I just want to show you that there is nothing to fear from me in the dungeon. If I awakened your body once to something you didn't think you could experience and want, I can awaken it again."

I'd gone still in his arms, my head resting in the crook of his neck. I didn't struggle against him, even though I wanted to. I still felt too weak and exhausted from everything that had already happened today. My pulse ratcheted up again to an unnatural pace as he carried me down the spiraling stairs to the dungeon.

The lights were still on from before.

He didn't put me down until he picked the contraption he wanted me on. "We'll stick with simple, this time," he said. I wasn't sure if simple would hurt more or less.

I didn't resist him when he helped me straddle a bench and lay forward over it. I was afraid whatever he was about to do would be much worse if I fought him. He took my wrists and then my ankles, each in turn, fastening them down in heavy metal. The sound of the locks clicking in place leeched the last bit of hope out of me.

Even without him touching me, I was immobile. Naked, spread out, tied down. Completely helpless, leaving his hands free to bring whatever torture on me he so desired.

"Shhhhh," he said. "You're okay. Everything is okay here." My body trembled under his touch as he stroked my back. "I'm just going to use the flogger on you today. Something light and easy. I'll work you up very slowly over time. There is nothing to fear here."

It didn't matter how many times he said it, I didn't believe it. He couldn't change reality and pain with only words. He moved away from me then, over to the nearest wall, and selected an instrument with a leather handle and several long leather pieces attached to it. I cringed and closed my eyes.

He made his way back over to me. I jumped, then settled when his hand stroked over my back again. "While I was out this morning, I dropped several messages in the ocean for your people. I'll keep trying until I get some kind of response. My intent isn't to keep you from ever seeing your family again." He swept my hair to the side out of his way. "We'll find some way for you to visit them. Maybe we'll take a boat out once we've established contact."

A tear slid down my cheek and dropped onto the stone floor. "Thank you, Master." I didn't understand how someone who could be so kind to me could have this in him. I was tempted to beg him again, thinking maybe I could reach him and gain mercy, but before I could open my mouth, the flogger came down on my back.

It was just once, then a long pause, as if he were letting me assemble the sensations and turn them over in my mind. I needed that processing time. Going from someone who was uncomfortable with simple human touch to being initiated into pain as a purported pleasurable activity was a big leap.

While my body had cringed away as the leather fell on it, it didn't feel like I'd anticipated. It was a more intense sensation than I was used to, but in honesty I couldn't define it as pain. The little leather fingers of the flogger were stimulating, warming, but not painful.

He did it again, and again, and again. Each time, the intensity and feelings slowly escalated, but they never got to a point where I couldn't tolerate it. Just a light sting and a warmth.

His hand stroked over my back again. "If you relax and accept it, the feeling will transform."

To what? It wasn't horribly painful, but the idea of relaxing my body while he hit me with anything was too foreign to assimilate, but I tried. I breathed slowly in and out, and closed my eyes. I thought of the sea and swimming alongside the dolphins. Anything to release the tension still curled inside me, as if I were only waiting for it to get worse somehow.

I managed to calm myself and the next time the flogger came down, my body was relaxed, loose. I gasped at the sensation skimming across my skin. Inexplicably I felt safe and warm and loved. These seemed like wrong emotions to have, but I couldn't help having them, all I could do was lie there as the feelings washed over me in waves.

"Better?" he asked.

"Yes, Master." When I relaxed, it was oddly almost pleasant. He kept it up, my back growing warmer as he continued. That was when the throb started between my legs.

It caught me off guard. I had intended to survive, to somehow endure whatever his strange tastes were. When it hadn't hurt too much, I'd felt relief. I hadn't expected to feel arousal or excitement. The idea that this could be mutually pleasurable and not just about him hadn't entered my mind.

"There it is," he said. As if he'd seen the thing inside me unfurl and completely accept and welcome this new form of pleasure.

He placed the flogger on the floor and moved behind me. With my legs spread and chained down, it was easy access. I felt completely at his mercy, grateful he *had* mercy. Glancing at the long row of increasingly scary implements on the wall, I knew he could easily do true damage if he wanted to, but that wasn't what he was about. This side of him fit perfectly with the patience he'd shown me.

Tears flowed down my cheeks, and I let out a moan as he entered me from behind, his body thrusting into mine in a steady, calming rhythm. It was a rhythm that hypnotized me and made me willing to do anything he wanted forever to be allowed this strange catharsis.

The orgasm bubbled from within me, from some place deep and sacred. His pleasure joined mine and it was as if we merged on a level I hadn't known before. As intense and frightening as humans had proven to be, there seemed to be infinite layers of sexual and emotional experience to be had with them.

As we both came down from the peak, he let himself fall forward over my back, his sweat-slicked skin resting against mine, his fingers threading through mine.

"Tell me you love me, Nerina."

"I love you, Master."

This time it was true.

THE KING'S PLEASURE

"*N*o! Please, please, no!"

At first the terrified screams seemed like remnants of a dream. Then it happened again, this time more urgent. The unrestrained begging was coming from down the hall. Surely Niall's guards knew better than to allow this kind of nonsense in the middle of the night. He threw the door open and sprinted toward the disruption.

There was no time for assessment. His eyes were only able to catch the glint of the sword in the torchlight as it came down.

"Stop!" he commanded. If his sleep was to be interrupted, he was going to get all the details before body parts were hacked off in his hallway.

The guard looked up, startled and more than a little guilty. Niall used the silence in the pause of activity and screaming to take in the scene before him. A peasant woman dressed in filthy rags was on the ground at the guard's feet, her arm caught in his death grip. Robert had clearly been about to cut off her hand.

When she looked up, her long, raven locks fell away from her face. The king almost took a step back in reaction to the brilliant green of her eyes and the trembling in her full lips. Tears tracked down her face, and he was already lost. He knew from her coloring and features that she was at least part gypsy, though not full. Not with those eyes.

"Well? Let her go," Niall said. "And sheath your sword. You'll have no use for it tonight."

The guard released the woman's wrist. A bruise was already forming, even against her darker flesh. He couldn't imagine what it would look like if she'd been fair like most of the maidens in the kingdom. She scrambled away from Robert on her hands and knees, ending against the wall just behind Niall. He wasn't sure if she'd moved instinctively behind him for his continued protection or if it was just the only place to go.

The guard genuflected and began to explain himself. "Your M—"

Niall cleared his throat. "You know how I feel about that at home." The king loathed the too-formal address and reserved it only for official business and formal occasions. Being awakened in the middle of the night by a screaming peasant was hardly a formal occasion.

"I'm sorry, sir. She was stealing from the castle."

Niall was unimpressed. The girl didn't strike him as a career criminal, despite the reputation of her people. If anything, she was wet behind the ears in that area, or she wouldn't have gotten caught.

"Stealing? What was she stealing? The crown jewels? My mother's good silver? You've aroused my curiosity now. So please, regale me. What priceless heirloom or artifact was she making off with?"

Robert reached behind him and picked up a loaf of bread that must have fallen to the ground in the scuffle.

"Bread? You disturbed my sleep with the intent to chop off her hand for *bread*?" If she'd risked breaking into the castle in the dead of night using God-only-knew-what means, her situation must be desperate, in which case Robert had more explaining to do.

"Surely you agree, sir, that she must be made an example of. Just getting into the castle is bad enough, but if she'd stolen anything and gotten away with it, it would weaken your authority."

"Why would she be stealing bread?"

"I'm sorry?" Robert said as if Niall hadn't enunciated clearly enough.

"Two days ago, I instructed you to take money from the treasury and feed the poor of the kingdom. I told you to make sure everyone had plenty of food to get them through the feast and festival this weekend. It's hardly appropriate to have a feast of plenty with starving subjects. Would you not agree?"

Robert looked at the ground. The money was missing from the treasury, so it had been taken. It just hadn't been used for the intended purpose.

"That's a very fine belt and shoes you have on," Niall remarked. "Quite a step up from what I issued you."

"I...um..." the guard stammered.

Niall crossed his arms over his chest. "So let me see if I properly understand things. I gave you an order to take money and feed the hungry; in direct violation of that order you go shopping. Perhaps we should chop off *your* hand. It seems appropriate considering the weight of your crime compared to hers. After all, that was what you'd intended for a far lesser offense."

"But she's a filthy gypsy!"

Niall nodded. "Yes. A filthy, hungry gypsy whom you stole from. You stole from me and you stole from her." He paused a moment, then shouted, "Guards!"

Several guards clad in the standard-issued uniform raced down the hallway at his command. His yell had likely awakened half the castle, but all bets were off once Niall had been disturbed. If he was up, he had no pity or concern for anyone else's sleep.

When the guards saw him they bowed low, then moved toward the gypsy. Of course, that would be their assumption. Why they felt he'd need to call in reinforcements with such a wisp of a girl, barely strong enough to stand under her own steam, he had no idea. Considering the battles he'd led them in, it was rather insulting. Just because they'd been in a long period of peace didn't mean he'd lost his edge.

"Don't touch the girl," he growled.

They backed away, each of their faces mirroring the same look of perplexity.

"Take Robert to the dungeon, and relieve him of his weapons, as well as the shoes and belt he stole from me. I'll decide his full punishment when I'm in a more gracious mood. I'm afraid what I'd offer him now wouldn't be very palatable for anyone."

The guards took their comrade and marched him off toward the dungeon, leaving Niall alone with the girl.

"Please, don't tell the king about this," she said, her voice so soft he had to strain to hear her. "You can have anything you want, just don't tell."

There was only one thing she had at her disposal to offer

him, considering she was so poor she had to attempt to steal a loaf of bread right from under his nose.

Niall wasn't surprised by her offer. He was, however, amused by her outburst. She didn't realize who he was. With his insistence on a more relaxed environment inside the castle and him in his nightclothes, how would she?

The girl had probably never been close enough to get a good look at the king, and certainly not in a sleeping robe and without his crown. He decided to play along for a minute.

"And why shouldn't I tell the king?"

"He'd probably kill me as soon as look at me," she said, her eyes wide and serious.

Niall's father had hated gypsies. He'd used every available excuse to kill or maim them, trying to slowly remove their kind entirely from the populace. Meanwhile, Niall had been off leading wars in which his father had been too old and feeble to act as anything but a figurehead. He'd only recently returned to take the throne at his father's passing. Of course, the girl couldn't know he wasn't like the former monarch.

His only similarity to his father was the desire to honor a single tradition. In the kingdom of Himeros, kings didn't marry. A harem of slaves was kept and the king chose an heir from the offspring that resulted. Niall had always desired a slave, though he wasn't sure how he felt about a full harem. Multiple women could only be trouble.

Women had a way of sliding past a man's defenses, manipulating with their charms. Observing the women presented for his approval, he'd seen the hunger for power that lit behind their eyes at the prospect of sharing the king's bed. It had caused him to put the whole business on hold, and thus far he hadn't taken even one slave. There was plenty of time for that once his throne was secure. He had cousins and brothers, should an heir not be available when he passed.

But now he had an idea brewing. A deliciously rebellious idea. What better way to end the feud with the gypsies than to create an heir that was part gypsy?

Besides, he couldn't set her free, now. As much as he was loath to admit it, Robert was right. Not about his feelings with regard to her kind, but about the weakness it would show to just release her. So it was her hand or her freedom.

The woman watched him, waiting to learn if he'd tell the king. Suddenly the game didn't seem as funny. Like others who didn't yet know him or his intentions toward the kingdom, she'd assumed he was a monster like his predecessor, that her life would be on the line if the king caught wind of her thievery. He couldn't imagine how hungry she must have been to take such a risk in the first place.

"I *am* the king."

The color drained out of her, nearly eradicating the olive in her complexion. Less than a second later, she was on her knees at his feet, her lips pressing against them. Her hair splayed across his bare skin as she shook violently. The act of fear and submission struck him with a sudden wave of arousal. If he hadn't already decided to keep her as his own, this moment would have been the deciding factor.

"Your Majesty..." It seemed she would say something else because of the way her voice trailed off, but it was as if she couldn't think of anything to fill the increasingly oppressive silence stretching between them, as if she feared begging for her life would only enrage him and ensure she lost it.

"What is your name?"

"A-Abigail."

"Not a very gypsy-like forename," he mused.

She cringed at that. "I'm only half-gypsy," she whispered, as if hoping that was enough to spare her.

"I see."

She jumped when he reached down and helped her to stand. "The floor is too cold for all of that out here. Come with me."

"Your Majesty?"

He gave her a long, hard look. "Oh no. You will call me Master."

Her eyes became as large as saucers at the implication. "You aren't going to kill me?"

His gaze swept over her. She needed to be cleaned up, but he was quite sure his grogginess wasn't overstating her loveliness. "Why would I kill something so beautiful that could bring me so much pleasure?"

She didn't reply as he led her back to his chambers; a guard was posted next to the entrance.

"John, wake the cook and have her reheat that pheasant with the roasted vegetables we had for lunch this afternoon, for two. I'd also like some bread and tea delivered." He paused in the open doorway and then turned as if in afterthought. "Oh, and I'll also need a slave garment." The guard's eyes widened, but he wisely bowed and moved down the hall to carry out the order.

ABIGAIL STOOD JUST INSIDE THE DOOR OF THE KING'S CHAMBER while he gave orders to the guard. This had to be some sort of trick. There was no possible way he'd spare her and take her as a slave. Not with her ancestry. Women in Himeros were groomed from puberty for such a position in the castle. Kings didn't take peasants off the street, definitely not peasants of her racial background. If she got pregnant, he'd never allow a gypsy—even as watered down as the bloodline would be by then—to be his heir.

So what was this, then? It had to be mere amusement. A cruel joke. He'd rape her and hurt her until he got bored. Then he'd have her killed or thrown back out on the streets. He was a war hero after all. He'd probably taken many women as spoils and played similar mind games with them.

Even though she knew what he must be planning, Abigail was determined to find a way to keep him amused as long as possible to delay her sentence. Maybe if enough time passed, she could gain his favor and be spared.

The door shut loudly behind the king. Even though his chambers were cavernous, the rooms shrank as the man in front of her seemed to fill every available bit of space with the power of his presence.

As he looked her over, she almost wished she hadn't been such a coward. She might have survived having her hand cut off, and the king wouldn't have been dragged out of bed. He would never have been the wiser about her foolish mission. But it hadn't just been about her. Her family was home waiting for something to eat. Now they'd have nothing except worry about what became of her.

"Come, let's get you cleaned up." His voice was gentle, like one might speak to a stray cat or a wounded bird, not what she'd expected at all.

He led her to a large bathroom. It seemed odd that he'd do this himself, rather than send her off to some servant to be bathed and groomed for him. But maybe it was the lateness of the hour that had him taking care of the chore instead, though he'd had no problem waking the cook.

"Abigail?" he prodded.

"Yes, Your...I mean...Master?"

"Don't look so terrified. Surely the life I can provide you is much better than the one you had. You'll have running water, electricity, fine clothes and perfume and jewels, plenty of food, and a secure roof over your head. Most women only fantasize about being in your position."

Abigail doubted that. Maybe if she hadn't been caught stealing from him, if she was fair-skinned and had been selected at some ceremony from a collected group of clean and eligible women from the kingdom. But not like this. He would show his monstrous side soon enough. Then he'd get rid of her and build his real harem. She was surprised he didn't have one yet. Why would he start with her?

She stood in the bathroom with her arms wrapped protectively around herself as he ran water in the tub, adding rich, fragrant oils and rose petals from a bowl nearby.

"Disrobe and shower the dirt off first." He pointed to the enclosed glass at the far side of the space. She looked down at the tiled floor to discover she was tracking dirt all over his bathroom, but he didn't seem to care.

"Servants will clean that. Do as I say."

She hesitated for a moment, her hands frozen at the hem of the dirty dress. Abigail wasn't sure if the garment could even properly be called a dress. It was a brown piece of shapeless fabric that covered her, with an old rope tied around the waist to give some attempt at adding shape or showing that she had one—something more than a rectangular blob of humanity.

If she'd been a full gypsy, she'd be in a colorful dress with sparkling jewelry. She would have lived in a caravan at the edge of the kingdom and would have danced and performed with the other women for coins in the street. She would have stolen—with expert precision—anything she needed. The gypsies were dancers and illusionists, and they often used their illusion to take what few would give them freely.

Abigail's dad was the gypsy of the family, the source of her olive complexion, the striking strength of her features, and her glossy, black hair. When he'd married outside the clan, he'd been banished from the tribe. Now she and her family could live in neither world. Gypsies and non-gypsies alike hated them, wishing they'd just die off and stop being such a nuisance.

"Abby."

She looked up sharply, shocked the king had shortened her name. Of course, he could call her whatever he wanted, it was just unexpected. It was what her family called her. She'd used her more formal name to put distance between herself and the situation she'd fallen into.

"Yes, Master?"

"Now. It's no time to be shy. I'll be careful with you your first time."

She winced. It wouldn't be her first time, and when there was no blood on the sheets, he'd know as well. Somehow she didn't think he'd appreciate the fact that she wasn't a virgin. Far from it. As sexually permissive as the kingdom was, there were still rules. Rules that were so unspoken and accepted that he'd just assumed her purity despite the logical likelihood that she was far removed from her virginity. Women groomed for the king's use got used by the king first.

She knew she must tell him the truth. If she didn't and he found out, he'd feel made a fool of. If she pleased him enough, he might change his mind about whatever awful end he'd planned for her. He might even let her go back to her family. But those odds were long if she lied by omission.

"I-I'm not a virgin." She squeezed her eyes shut, bracing herself for his reaction, waiting for the illusion of mercy to evaporate. She flinched when she felt his warm hand resting softly on her cheek.

"Then why are you so shy?"

Abigail opened her eyes, surprised when she found no anger in his features. He didn't seem to care about the matter one way or the other.

Of course he would assume general shyness and nothing more. How could he understand the swirl of emotions running through her? After all, he was the king. He was rich, powerful, and beautiful. His hair was a golden blond that made him look like a god straight from Mt. Olympus. His eyes were gray, but instead of being cold, like she'd expect from such a color, they were warm and kind. Had his eyes been like that the whole time tonight? She hadn't dared to look into them, too afraid of the disgust and loathing she might find. Was there a chance it wasn't a trick?

She shrugged in response to his question. "I'm afraid you might not be pleased by what you see." It was the first thing she'd thought to say, but there was a measure of truth locked inside the words. She was afraid of doing anything to add to any abuse he might heap on her simply for not being fair like the acceptable members of Himeros. She'd been reminded on a daily basis almost since birth of just how unacceptable she was, a stain on the kingdom that no one could wash out.

"I'm sure that won't be the case." The king brushed the pad of his thumb against her cheek. It was such a sweet, intimate gesture that she sucked in a breath and allowed herself to have the fantasy for just a moment. What if he really meant it? What if he really wanted her?

Selfish, Abigail. So selfish. Tears began to race down her cheeks. How could she enjoy a rich life in the castle while her family starved and died in the streets? She closed her eyes and took a shaky breath. Right now her only concern had to be making sure the king didn't regret his choice to spare her from the guard's blade.

She gripped the hem of the fabric and pulled it over her head. As the cloth hit the ground, she looked up, self-conscious. He stared intensely for a moment, so intensely that she felt far more innocent than she was. It took all her willpower to refrain from covering herself from his gaze, but he wouldn't like such an overt display of willfulness or modesty. It didn't fit with the local culture and it would be another reminder of how alien she truly was to him. After a few minutes, he nodded his approval and pointed again to the glass door.

A fresh bar of lavender and oat soap sat on the shelf in the shower. She'd never seen one before—the shower, not soap. She'd seen soap. Only the richest people in the kingdom had running water. She'd never seen running water, aside from the fountains outside the castle, but that had been more decorative than functional.

Words were scrawled above the handle on each side of the faucet. Abigail guessed it told people which side was hot and which was cold, but she couldn't read the words to know for sure. She tested each side and fiddled with the handles until she found the right temperature. It was another indication of how different she was from the types of women kings usually took for their harems. On top of everything else, they were formally educated. The only category she fit neatly into was beauty. She may be poor, but she'd seen the way men looked at her.

She lathered up and watched the dirt and grime as it swirled down the drain. God, she was disgusting. All that dirt. It was like she never bathed. She did, in fact. It was just that she'd been out all day and into the night. She'd tried several methods of acquiring food, from searching through the forest, to looking for an easier mark to steal from. No good opportunities had presented themselves, and she'd been desperate. She'd been about to turn to prostitution—assuming she could beguile a man in such a state—when she'd seen a back gate to the castle had been left open for a late night delivery.

It had been insane and suicidal, but she knew if any place had food, it would be the castle, and surely they wouldn't miss a few loaves of bread, not with so much available to eat. If she could pass through undetected...but then it hadn't happened that way. The second her hand had touched the bread, a bright spotlight had flicked on, bathing her in a frighteningly unnatural light.

Only the castle and the highest nobles had electric lights. To everyone else, the technology was forbidden. The power of the humming electric light had dazed her for a moment, and she almost got caught by the guard.

She'd quickly gotten hold of herself and darted through the castle, hoping to lose her pursuer in the maze of hallways. Inside, electricity had been abandoned for the older torch-light. With the high, stone walls and good ventilation, the torches posed no problems to the air they breathed. It had felt more familiar, and in that familiarity, she'd found a burst of speed. But it hadn't been fast enough or soon enough to elude him.

Abigail shut the water off and opened the door, cool air hitting her and jolting her back to the present moment, a decidedly better moment than the one with the guard. For now at least.

"You'll find a towel to your left."

She blushed and took the towel off the hook. The shower door was a crystal clear glass that left nothing to the imagination. He'd stood and watched each drop of water as it slid over her curves, pressing into all the places his hands would soon stroke. She wrapped the towel around her and looked down, trying to avoid the penetration of his gaze. When she was dry, she made her way over to the tub and got in, never raising her eyes to his.

The fragrances coming off the water were a blend of jasmine, rose, and gardenia, with a touch of sandalwood. She'd been exposed to each of these smells on the few occasions she'd been allowed inside the perfumery, when the shopkeeper's son, Bryant, had worked. Inevitably, after only a few whiffs of perfumes, his father had shooed her out.

But she'd kept coming back. Eventually, she'd lost her virginity to Bryant, and in return he'd taught her about perfume and what each scent was. Like her mother, he wasn't afraid of the gypsies and seemed intrigued by Abigail's exotic background and looks.

She'd had no illusions they would marry, but he'd been a nice break from the cold reality of her life. He'd intended to teach her to read when the shopkeeper had found out and sent him away to another city, presumably on business. Abigail suspected Bryant would have been disinherited if he'd kept the relationship going. The last thing she wanted was for him to end up like her, on the fringes of society, barely tolerated even as a beggar.

The king pulled up a stool to sit and brush her hair. It was such an intimate gesture; the menial nature of the task seemed far beneath royalty. It felt so wrong that it took all her willpower not to pull away. She could barely remember the last time someone had brushed her hair. She'd been a small child. Five, maybe six. In some ways she felt like that again: small, vulnerable, but also cared for. She hoped it would last.

The dizzying smells and warmth from the bath and the softness of the rose petals as they drifted against her skin made her believe the king wasn't like his father. If his intention was to harm her, he would have ordered her into the shower, then thrown her down and had his way with her. He wouldn't be sitting beside the tub brushing her hair, using the good oils in her bath. Even Abigail knew that much.

She sighed and sagged against the tub, finally letting the last bits of anxiety slide out of her. Then she thought of her family again, and the tears came back.

"I'm not going to hurt you." His voice was a deep sound she could happily listen to for eons as it rumbled over her.

"I know." It wasn't a lie. Somehow she *did* know. "It's my family. They'll be worried. They're waiting for me to bring food."

"Don't fret about them. I'll take care of it."

Abigail tensed again, but there was nothing sinister in his tone. A knock sounded on the main chamber door, shattering her thoughts. The king left her alone, and she leaned against the tub, taking in her surroundings.

Candles lined the walls, but all of them were unlit. Abigail stretched and looked at the designs on the ceiling and the light-colored stone of the walls around her. Cool air blew inside through a vent. Only the rich had the power or the right to control the temperature of the air indoors. It felt obscene and decadent, as if they were playing god by over-coming the power of the weather.

The king returned several minutes later and held out a robe. "Dinner is here."

In her fear and panic, Abigail's hunger had briefly disap-peared. Now it came back as an angry gnawing feeling that seemed to climb out of her stomach all the way up to claw at the back of her throat, demanding satisfaction. The feeling made her light-headed, and she had trouble standing on her own.

"Careful now," he said, grabbing her elbow to steady her. His touch on her arm felt strong and stable. Despite the situa-tion, it felt like safety. If she could stay on his good side, she was convinced nothing could ever harm her. She wanted to feel his powerful arms around her. She wanted to feel shielded from the outside world for the first time, cocooned in the peace and warmth of the castle.

She hid the unexpected flood of emotion at such a simple gesture with a weak smile as she stepped out of the tub, and the moment dissipated like the steam rising off the water.

She gratefully put on the robe. The king pulled the plug on the water and headed back into the main room. Abigail trailed behind him, trying not to linger in the memory of his touch.

She shouldn't long so deeply for his hands to be on her, should she? In person, he seemed so counter to all she'd heard about him. She'd expected him to be vicious and ruth-lessly violent, but the way he'd been with her had been a tempered, gentle kind of strength. It was hard to reconcile that image with the way he'd been in war.

Next to the bed was a table with two soft, high-backed red chairs. The king pulled a chair back for her and she sat, feeling awkward and strange accepting an almost subservient gesture from the top tier of royalty. To hide her discomfort, she focused instead on the two glimmering silver domes on the table.

The king made no comment. He sat across from her and removed the coverings to reveal the food. She couldn't remember the last time she'd tasted meat, or even vegetables. Mostly her diet had been stale bread, water from a nearby stream, and a few roots and berries.

Even as hungry as she was, she stared at it for a long time, not daring to believe it was real. She was certain she'd soon awaken on the pallet in the corner of the small hut her family shared. But a minute passed and then two, and she didn't wake up.

"Eat," he said.

Abigail didn't have to be told twice. She began tentatively, dipping a piece of the bread in the sauce drizzled over the vegetables. She looked up, unsure if this was improper, but he didn't seem fazed or bothered by how she ate.

A soft moan escaped her lips. She'd never had food this good. The weakness that had eternally lived inside each muscle was fading already—even with just a few bites of truly good food. If he fed her like this every day she could imagine having energy and vitality, actually feeling good for a change, instead of like an old hag trapped in the body of a much younger woman.

When she finally finished the meat and vegetables, she looked up to find the king had been finished for awhile. He sat with his arms crossed over his chest, observing her.

"Thank you, Master," she said almost automatically. Giving him the address he wanted was so easy, so natural to her that she briefly fantasized belonging to him had

somehow been her destiny. She had a feeling she'd be
thanking him for every little crumb he threw her way.

The king pushed his chair back, and Abigail's gaze
followed as he went to the bed, her eyes widening at the sight
of the clothing. She'd been so hungry she hadn't noticed it. It
must have been brought in with the food.

She'd seen slave girls dancing for the last king during
festivals held in the open square. But she'd only seen the
women from a distance, always careful to stay hidden on the
fringes so she wouldn't be spotted by the gypsy-hating
monarch. She'd been in love with the garments the harem
wore from the moment she first saw them glistening in the
brightness of the day.

The tops were like the fancy ladies' undergarments
Abigail had heard the rich women wore under their dresses.
They were encrusted with thousands of colorful beads and
tiny jewels that reflected brilliantly in the sunlight making
them look like goddesses. The tops cinched their breasts
together, displaying ample cleavage. Their bellies had been
bare with a single gold and diamond chain that went around
each of their waists.

The chain wasn't merely decorative. It displayed their
status, that they were the personal property of the king and
only to be touched by others with his permission, which he
tended to give freely to nobles and visiting dignitaries. The
rumor was that the slaves liked being passed around. And
why shouldn't they? No one inside the upper echelon of the
kingdom had ever been brainwashed with the idea that sex or
nudity was dirty or shameful, or even particularly private.

Just below the navel was a similarly bead and jewel-
encrusted belt. From the bottom of the belt hung hundreds of
strands of beads and jewels, along with a few ribbons of rich

brocade fabric interspersed at various intervals in between. When they moved, their legs cut through the strands of beads and fabric like a parting curtain. On their wrists and ankles were matching gold and diamond chains. Their throats remained bare of ornamentation because only the noble free women wore necklaces.

When she was a little girl, before she'd really understood who these women were and what they did for the king, she'd wanted to be one of them. Her father had gotten angry, saying that no gypsy woman would ever debase herself in such a manner, no matter how honored the position was in the local culture.

She'd never mentioned it again, feeling shame rather than the old awe whenever she caught a glimpse of the women.

The garment and jewelry on the king's bed was a jade green that would bring out her eyes. He picked up the clothing and draped it carefully over a chaise lounge in the corner.

"You will wear this tomorrow. Someone will attend to your bath and help you dress after breakfast. Tonight you'll have no need for clothing."

Abigail swallowed hard around the lump forming in her throat. Of course she'd have no need for clothing.

He offered his hand, and she took it and stood. She held herself still as a statue as he pushed the robe off her shoulders and let it fall in a whoosh to the floor. Although he'd watched her walk naked to the shower and observed her as she'd bathed for him, there had been an activity for her to focus on then. Now it was just her body and his eyes drinking in her curves.

"Lie down on the bed."

She carefully climbed the steps beside the ornate bed.
She tried not to sigh at how firm yet comfortable it was. The
sheets and blankets were so soft, she couldn't imagine how
the king got up in the morning. In her head he was always *the
king*. Before he'd taken the throne and had led their people in
battles, he'd been *the prince*. She was aware his name was
Niall, but she couldn't bring herself to think of him by
anything other than a title. It felt too intimate even lying in
his bed.

She wanted to ask what he'd meant by taking care of her
family and when he might do it. He could mean anything, but
she hoped he intended something benevolent. If they could
just get a regular delivery of bread, she'd be grateful. She was
afraid one of her brothers or sisters or her parents would get
too weak or sick and die without proper nourishment soon.
Although she couldn't help, given the circumstances, she felt
guilty they were starving while her belly was full and finally
content.

Abigail tried not to gawk as the king undressed. She could
never forget he'd led battles or the reputation that had
followed him in his conquests. His thighs were thickly corded
with muscles, and his stomach, chest, and arms were the
same. When he turned away from her, she took in a sharp
breath at the impressive expanse of his back. He chuckled in
response.

The king had many scars, clearly from battle. One
wrapped around his stomach to end at his lower back. It was
the type of injury that should have killed him.

Abigail wondered how much worse her situation might
be now if he'd died in that battle and a king less merciful had
been awakened in the middle of the night by her screams.
She couldn't imagine things would have played out this way.

She was still having difficulty reconciling the ideas she'd had about him before, when the prince was said to be vicious on the battlefield. She'd imagined someone cruel and unforgiving like his father. Whatever he may be in war, it didn't seem to extend to his bedroom.

Abigail's gaze finally landed between his legs. He was already firm and hard, leaving no question as to his desire for her. Although she wasn't a virgin, the few lovers she'd entertained weren't as large. He was both longer and had more girth than she remembered encountering, and it made her a little nervous, worried she wouldn't be able to accommodate him without pain.

When he touched her, it was with such possession that if she'd doubted he truly meant to keep her, she held no such uncertainty now. From the moment his fingers dug into her hip and his mouth closed around her breast, she knew she belonged to him. It wasn't his pronouncement that made her his, it was the possession in his eyes and in the way in which he held her. It was something inside him that called out to the thing inside her that longed for that possession even as she feared it.

Her fantasies of being one of the king's women came back now, blooming to life in spite of her father's disapproval. Only this king wasn't old and past his prime. He was still young and strong and in control.

If it had been anyone but this man, she might have felt in some way violated, but the certainty of his ownership was so complete and the improved accommodations and food were so drastic, that it didn't once cross her mind that she was being taken against her will. Her only fear, besides his size, was that it wasn't real or that he would turn dark and cruel on her. As his fingers kneaded her breast and he kissed the hollow of her neck, those fears began to shrivel and die.

He tore his mouth from her throat. "Open to me." His voice was a low, commanding growl that she couldn't imagine not obeying. Her legs fell open and she gasped as fingers pressed inside her, drawing out moisture, then plunging in again for more as if he wanted to coat himself with as much of her as possible.

His invasion was delicious and decadent much as the bath and food had been. The more his fingers squirmed inside her body, the wetter she became in response.

After several minutes of this stimulation, her hips arched off the bed, and she began to pant, seeking her pleasure in earnest. He must have sensed the shift in her reactions, that she was climbing toward her orgasm, because he pulled his fingers away suddenly.

"Not yet, little one. I want you to beg me for it."

She felt her whole body flush with embarrassment. What was happening between them was mild and probably nothing compared to his dark and perverted appetites, but she hadn't been trained or raised for this. Why hadn't he taken a woman who'd been properly trained? Everything about his touch felt richer, darker, more wanton in light of the knowledge that she wasn't his equal, that she couldn't just stop things and walk away.

Her other lovers hadn't teased, nor had they spoken, except prior to the event to whisper the endearments neces- sary to get her clothes off—the magic incantation to part a woman's thighs. Men recited it shamelessly to meet their carnal needs. This man would never utter such a pointless litany; he would merely possess what was his to take by divine right.

She looked away, the intensity of the moment becoming too much to tolerate. "Please... I-I can't."

The king's eyes turned stormy. "You can't? I saved you from amputation, fed you, bathed you, gave you a roof, and you... can't?" His voice hadn't risen, but the quiet command and condescending amusement made her afraid. It was as if he found her small rebellion adorable but intended to disabuse her of her notion of choices. No one had choices in the king's presence. They obeyed or they suffered whatever consequences he deemed appropriate.

Stupid, Abigail. What did she mean she couldn't? He could have her executed for looking at him weirdly, and no one in the kingdom would try to stop it. They'd say, "Good riddance to bad rubbish," and rejoice in the streets.

The king flipped Abigail onto her stomach, startling her. The cry that came out of her mouth wasn't from the sudden change in position, but from his hand coming down across her ass. He spanked her hard, his hand landing in quick, brutal succession, until she broke and the tears poured out of her.

"Please...please..."

He continued his assault on her flesh until she went boneless, her body giving into it, even if her voice still whimpered and pleaded.

"Good. Now beg for pleasure."

Abigail still lay on her stomach, in shock, her wet cheek pressed against the bedsheets as he rubbed where he'd just struck her, soothing away the pain.

She closed her eyes. "Please let me come, Master."

"Was that so hard? I'll allow it, but you have to be the one to do it, now. Put your hand between your legs and rub yourself for me."

He adjusted her body so that her ass was raised in the air. Her pussy was exposed, leaving nothing to his imagination, giving him a view that humiliated her. She wondered if he understood she wasn't raised like this. She hadn't been indoctrinated into their kingdom's cultural attitudes about sex. She wasn't as open and free as the others were. Abigail didn't know if he even knew, or if he'd care if he did.

"Stroke yourself." He was becoming impatient.

Though she was embarrassed and a little afraid of him now—as well as what his future sexual demands might be—she slipped her fingers between her thighs to obey. After a few minutes, she forgot the voyeuristic king as she pressed herself harder against her hand, her pleasure mounting higher.

As she touched herself, she perversely replayed the earlier scene in the hallway. She came as she re-imagined the moment he'd revealed he was the king, and she'd knelt and kissed his feet. It was a mystery why that horrid moment was the one that sent her over the edge into completion, but something about that extreme moment of fear heightened all her senses.

She didn't have time to feel shame or worry about what might be wrong with her, because as soon as she came, he was behind her. His cock shoved past her entry, which had tightened from lack of use. She might have expected her body to recoil in revulsion. Instead, the excited flip in her stomach betrayed her as he buried himself deeper, his, fierce, animalistic thrusts revealing his own recent sexual drought.

He gripped her shoulder as he spilled inside her. His grip was so hard she feared she'd be a bruised mess by morning. As he tried to catch his breath, he said, "Are you sure you weren't a virgin?"

When she didn't reply, he rolled over and pulled her against him, covering them both with the blankets. His lips pressed tenderly against her forehead. The moment was fleeting, but she wanted to hold onto it forever.

"Sleep," he said.

The king was asleep within minutes. For Abigail it took over an hour. It was far too loud inside her head, and she couldn't shut off the thoughts. The last conscious realization that drifted through her mind was that her bottom was still warm and sore from his hand.

AFTER ONE NIGHT WITH ABBY IN HIS BED, NIALL FOUND himself already attached. It had been far too long since he'd been with a woman. But that wasn't the only thing that had made him so possessive of her in such short time. There was something real in her fear and desperation to please him, something that had been missing in the meticulously trained women presented for his harem. He hadn't felt that spark with any of them, hadn't felt any real submission. They behaved by rote, like well-trained sexual robots. Maybe another man would have been satisfied with that, but the king hadn't been.

He'd quickly sent them away and determined to avoid the matter of a harem for a while. After all, he had a kingdom to get in order and no experience leading anything other than an army.

His time at war came back to him in crisp detail. The only thing that lay before him now was the mission. And the mission was keeping his new prize safe. Most of the court and the kingdom would fall in line on his say-so, even if they didn't like it and gossiped privately amongst themselves. But there could still be open resistance. Part of him hoped for the opportunity to take a swift and firm stand.

When he'd awakened that morning and glanced over at his slave's sleeping form, he'd known he'd made a good choice. Far from his tiredness overemphasizing her beauty the night before, it had diminished it. She was even lovelier in the light of morning than he'd thought. And her small, warm body pressed trustingly next to his had given him the best night's rest of his life, not to mention the perfect way they had fit together when he'd taken her for the first time.

His thoughts drifted to the spanking. Though he wanted to show her kindness, he wouldn't allow his slave to mistake it for weakness. She needed to understand she would obey his requests the first time every time, no exceptions. Hesitation or refusal would earn her punishment of whatever nature he desired. The sooner she learned, the more smoothly their relationship would go.

He'd cleared the court for his early morning business. He'd had her family brought in soon after sunrise and fed a hearty breakfast before being brought in to see him. If Abigail's state of malnourishment was any indication, they'd be too hungry to properly hear him otherwise.

The family was ushered in, their faces painted with apprehension, despite the fullness of their stomachs. With the mother and father were two young boys, perhaps around eight or nine—twins from the look of it—a girl that was only a few years younger than Abigail, and a female toddler.

Most of the children had their gypsy father's swarthy looks with dark complexion and hair, but the youngest girl was blonde and fair like her mother. Everyone but the toddler bowed appropriately. Instead of bowing, the youngest throat in a possessive pose that demonstrated her as his undisputed property. Then he addressed his audience.

"Himeros was founded and built to worship the gods of lust, our patrons who have blessed us with so much wealth and hedonistic pleasure. On the final night of the high festival in their honor, I formally introduce my property, Abigail."

He leaned down and whispered in her ear. "As my slave, you're the symbol of the evening. Surrender yourself completely."

The king noted the light trembling in her body as he guided her to straddle the bench and mount the phallus. It was the first time she'd been on display in front of this many people, all attention fully on her. She let out a whimper as she lowered onto the thick, cold metal object. When it was firmly seated inside her, Abigail leaned forward and began to ride it, her tempo matching that of the drumbeats until she and the drums seemed to merge into one thing.

Whistles and cat calls came up from the crowd as the sexual energy rose higher.

"Fuck it until you come for us," Niall growled. He'd moved behind her, rubbing her back and squeezing her breasts as she rode the phallus harder. The simple display was pure ritual to their gods; her exposed body the sacrifice, her orgasm, the offering.

A few minutes passed before she let out a moan that reverberated around the grounds. When she finished, Niall motioned for two nearby guards to help him move her for the final part of the ceremony. The festival attendees formed a line at the bottom of the stage as Abby was pulled off the phallus, her cum dripping down the metal.

He ran his finger through it, then put it to his mouth,

girl gave him a toothy grin, not having the faintest notion of who he was, nor caring. She'd just had roast pork and eggs and biscuits with gravy for breakfast, so in her eyes, he was her friend. He hoped the rest of the family would feel that way soon enough.

"Please don't look so anxious," Niall said. He wasn't sure why it bothered him to see Abigail's family looking at him with such abject terror. He could understand why they might fear being brought in to see the king given the history of attacks on their kind by his father. "If I'd intended to harm you, would I have fed you first?"

The features on the adults' faces seemed to relax by a small measure, acknowledging the logic therein.

Niall didn't waste any time. "I'm giving you a house and land. It's fifteen bedrooms, a parlor, a kitchen, a dining room, a ballroom, three bathrooms, and a conservatory, as well as a large and gracious entry hall. There is a well-kept garden in the back and stables with horses. Your servants will greet you when you arrive and take care of anything you need. The land is thirty-two acres. You'll also be given a generous allowance to take care of any expenses for the house, food, clothing, and whatever else you care to purchase."

The family stared at him for a moment, their eyes a little unfocused. It was as if the king had dropped a boulder on their heads instead of giving them a generous gift.

"Traditionally, 'Thank you, Your Majesty,' is the proper reply," the king said.

"But, Your Majesty, why?" The father looked at him as if he wasn't quite sure it was all real and that he wasn't still asleep.

The doors at the back of the room opened, and Abigail entered in the green-jeweled slave garment. Her hair had been piled up and pinned on the top of her head like a Greek goddess.

Niall took a deep breath at the sight of her and adjusted his clothing so he wouldn't look like an uncontrolled teenage boy getting his first taste of pussy. No one had ever looked so radiant in beads and jewels. The green made her eyes even more spectacular, and her dark, olive skin made the jewels seem to sparkle even brighter in contrast.

Abigail had excellent timing. He gestured for her with a flick of his fingers. She didn't make eye contact with her family as she walked up to him. Niall found that a little odd but made no comment. He snapped and pointed at the cushion beside his feet, and she knelt.

He stroked the back of her neck languidly. "Because Abigail is mine, and so I've chosen to make sure her family is well cared for."

The father's face went dark. "I don't care who you are. If you think we'll live in luxury as payment for our daughter whoring herself out to you, you don't know who you're dealing with."

Well, that was unexpected.

"Emilian, don't," his wife begged.

"You should listen to her," Niall said calmly, still stroking Abigail's skin. The muscles in her neck and shoulders had tensed considerably in the past few seconds. He was glad he'd chosen to do this part privately. If he had to make an example of someone, he didn't want it to have to be a member of her family.

"And just so matters are clear," Niall continued, "you aren't being paid for prostituting your daughter. She wasn't given a choice. She was caught stealing bread to feed you. Would you have preferred that I sent her back to you relieved of one of her hands? No one steals from me and walks free without paying a price. This is her price."

Emilian's eyes hadn't softened. If possible they'd become sharper. There was murder in his gaze. If the king had been anybody else and hadn't been surrounded by guards, he imagined he'd already be on the floor in a pool of his own blood.

"It would be better than her shaming the family as a whore," the father said. "You may think gypsies are that way, but you know nothing. It is not how I raised my daughter to be."

"Emilian!" the wife hissed, her eyes filling with increasing terror.

Niall could hear Abigail's quiet crying, and almost regretted bringing her in for this. He hadn't guessed it would play out this way. Typically, it was an honor to be brought into the king's harem, not an insult. This was especially true of the woman chosen first, whose status was hardly different than that of a queen in other kingdoms.

Most queens were little more than slaves when you thought about it. As long as there existed a king, her power was whatever he indulged her with. Was honesty in labels not a better thing than polite lies? He'd always been proud that Himeros was open and free in ways other kingdoms weren't, that citizens were able to partake in and enjoy the pleasures of the flesh without irrational guilt or shame coming over them.

"I'm sorry you feel that way, but your daughter hasn't *whored herself* as you so tactfully put it. This is the highest position for a woman in this kingdom. It will result in an heir that is part gypsy. It will end the feuding. She didn't choose this. I did. She is my property with absolutely no say in the matter. So if you want to be angry with someone, be angry with me, but be careful with how you express it. I'm still the king and who you are to her is the only reason you aren't in the dungeon. I'm giving you all this because it's proper and because I can't allow my slave's family to starve. It wouldn't be right. You will be escorted to your new dwelling and a tailor and seamstress will be at your disposal by this afternoon. Don't come to court or the castle again without an invitation, for your sake as well as your daughter's. And when you *are* invited, I suggest you conduct yourself more cordially."

Niall waved a hand, the doors opened, and the family was escorted out. When he was alone with Abigail, the king made eye contact with the head guard. "Leave us and allow no one in."

John arched a brow but bowed and led the men out into the hallway.

ABIGAIL TENSED, FEARING SOME SORT OF PUNISHMENT WAS coming, though she couldn't figure out what she could have done to offend the king.

He patted the chaise beside him. "Come, sit and talk with me."

With his help, she rose from the cushion and moved to where he'd directed her. The throne room was different than that of many kingdoms. Most had two thrones: a large one for the king and a smaller one for the queen. In Himeros, there was only one throne. It had one armrest instead of two. On the right, the space where the armrest would have been was open, and attached to the throne was a chaise upon which the most favored slave—or the most favored slave of the moment—reclined, her head resting on the king's lap.

Abigail lay across the chaise, relaxing only when his fingers threaded soothingly through her hair. He didn't seem angry with her. Still, she didn't understand why he'd make her suffer through her family's visit.

"Tell me what all that was about. Why would your family react that way? Why wouldn't they be honored that I chose you? For god's sake, I didn't just choose you, I took you first. Possibly exclusively. Most parents would be effusive with their gratitude and pride."

"We're not that way," she said quietly, still afraid of enraging the king. "Are you going to get rid of me?"

"Of course not. You're mine whether your family approves or not. I'm just trying to understand."

She'd always known Himeros was a permissive society, at least from the time she'd finally figured out what slave girls did. The kingdom was known for its perversions, and tended to attract travelers and foreign leaders who wanted to get away from the repressive propriety of their own kingdoms. All the feasts and festivals were orgies after dark for the adults that remained.

"When my father and mother married, he was shut off from the tribe. The gypsies stay on the fringes. I guess they're always assumed to be laid back with regards to sexuality, but they're pretty private. And they aren't welcome in the culture, anyway, so there isn't much exposure to it. Because my father was shut off from the tribe and my mother was cut off from everyone else, we've been outcasts from both groups. I've been raised to see everything that happens in court as dirty and immoral. There is no way my family can ever see things in the same way others in the kingdom do. I'm not even sure if I can. We have a sense of modesty you don't have—and maybe can't even comprehend."

There was a bit of an edge to the king's voice when he replied, an edge Abigail wished she could erase. "If our ways disgust you so much, why hasn't your family packed up and moved elsewhere?"

"It's not so easy when you have no money. We can't just leave. Even if we did, gypsies aren't welcomed in many other places, either. We'd face the same social problems. I think this was easier for my parents. My father likes being able to look down on something he disapproves of in the people who look down on him. Please don't be angry with me. I can't help how I was raised. They can't help that they were shut off from everyone. How can you begin to understand a culture that pushes you out? Of course we'd react differently."

"And do you hold the same extreme feelings of disgust toward our ways?"

She didn't say anything. It felt too exposing to be draped across his lap in a slave garment with his guards standing just outside. If she'd been wearing something else or had been in a different setting, perhaps it wouldn't be so uncomfortable, but she felt foolish being here, dressed like this, when she didn't fit into their ways at all. She felt like a ridiculous prude in his presence and thought he must think the same thing.

Secretly, Abigail had considered the permissiveness of Himeros to be liberating, or at least potentially so. She wished she didn't understand the concept of shame being linked and mixed with sex. She wished she could erase her upbringing so she could be as free as the women she'd caught glimpses of as they'd danced for the king.

His hand drifted from her hair to part the strands of beads and jewels. He caressed her bottom, his fingers moving lewdly between her cheeks. He was pushing her buttons, testing her. She squirmed uncomfortably, even though there was no one to see the exchange.

"I'm not letting you go. I don't care how you were raised. You'll learn," he said.

Her breath hitched in her throat as he touched her. It was as if her body had lain dormant, waiting for the right man to come along and awaken her to her erotic potential. Every touch, every caress, no matter how lewd or invasive heated her from somewhere deep within. She wondered if he'd share her with visiting nobles as was custom. The thought made her heart thump hard in her chest, and she prayed he'd show her mercy when men started asking for her, even though a part of her grew wet over the idea.

Finally he stopped fingering her. "Sit up."

Abigail obeyed the order, afraid of what might be coming next, but he simply gathered her in his arms, adjusting her so she sat on his lap. Then he guided her head to rest on his shoulder and held her, rubbing her back.

"You will be exquisite. I'll train you, and in time this shyness and discomfort will go away. Your wishes will not factor into my choices, however, I want to know where you are right now. If it's possible, do you want me to take your inhibitions away?"

With her face pressed against the king's neck, she felt safer. "Yes, Master."

"Have you always had these feelings of discomfort and repulsion about our ways?"

She knew he felt her head shake against his shoulder. But for some reason she felt compelled to explain her reply. "When I was little, I wanted to grow up and be one of the king's harem. I didn't know what a harem was then. I just knew I thought they were beautiful and free, and I wanted to feel like that. But my father got angry and yelled at me when I said something about it. He told me those women were bad people, and it was shameful to want to be like them. So I pushed the feelings away because I didn't want to be bad."

"Oh, Abby," he said, sighing.

It felt like the world stopped while he held her, everything pausing in that sad sigh. She wished they could stay like this forever, alone in this room away from everyone, but too soon a knock interrupted the private moment of sanctuary.

"Enter," the king said.

It was John. "I'm sorry to disturb you, sir, but our guests have arrived."

"Send in the members of court and we'll get started."

Abigail's stomach churned as the doors opened and several high-ranking members of the king's court filed in, followed by a few guards.

They all bowed and waited patiently for the king's address, not hiding the curiosity in their gazes at the sight of the new addition to court.

"I will be formally introducing my slave to the kingdom at the feast and festival tomorrow night. A royal proclamation will go out this afternoon. Abigail, stand here beside me and let them all get a good look at you."

She stood shakily and turned to face the court. The king slipped his hand into hers and squeezed. She was grateful for the small offering of support and comfort. Then he stood behind her. His hands moved around to her front and he began stroking over her breasts and belly and between her thighs. It was a proprietary touch as if to say: "Look at what's mine."

She closed her eyes, but he whispered in her ear, "Look at them, Abby. Look at how much they desire you."

His voice was kind; his intent, clear. He was doing what he said he'd do, stripping away her inhibitions, peeling back the stifling layers that had held her captive to other people's discomforts. She forced her eyes open. Though not all of them looked happy to see the king had taken a gypsy, most had clear lust and admiration in their eyes. It sent an unexpected wave of arousal between her legs.

The king continued to casually run his hands over her as he spoke. "She will be treated with the same respect as any other pleasure slave. She will only be touched in any way with my permission. As my personal property, she ranks higher than all of you. If I hear anyone has said or done anything malicious toward her or her family, there will be heavy consequences. You can also expect legislation within the month that prohibits unprovoked attacks on any gypsy."

Abigail sucked in a breath. The nervous tension in the air was thick, and she wasn't sure it was all hers. She'd heard being the king's slave was a position that was honored, but she really hadn't understood it was this extreme. In another kingdom, would that have made her the queen? Maybe not. Other kingdoms wouldn't have displayed the queen as a sexual object. She wished she didn't find all of this so foreign when others were at ease. It didn't seem to occur to anyone else to link a sexually open and available woman with anything shameful or bad.

"This is an outrage!" one of the men said. "You can't take a gypsy. You'll make a mockery out of Himeros!"

"Careful, Mark," the king said.

"No! Take my title if you like. I won't stand behind something like this. Others will side with me. This is unacceptable even for us."

Abigail craned her neck to look up at the king, expecting anger, but instead she saw... triumph?

"Why don't I take your life instead?"

"On what grounds?" the man shouted, seemingly unaware of how his situation had deteriorated.

"Treason against your king, of course. Do you think my father would have stood for such a mutinous outburst? When I make a proclamation, everyone falls in line. Or else. Guards, take him. Today's proceedings will be reported in the official proclamation so there is no confusion about my feelings. I wouldn't want to have to quietly kill half the kingdom to get my point across."

Two guards came out of the crowd of nobles and grabbed the man's arms, dragging him out of the room. Mark dug his heels in and screamed obscenities.

The king sighed. "This is not your first breech of loyalty, and you know it. But it is your last." He turned to one of the other guards. "Please show our festival guests in. They must be very tired from their journey."

Abigail stared in horror as the man was taken away. Her impression of the king's mercy was fading fast. It was impossible to reconcile the previous night's kindness, as well as the tenderness he'd shown her only a few minutes ago in private, with the way he was behaving now. How easily he could dispense with a life.

She looked back at him, and he caught her gaze. Surely all her feelings of betrayal were shining out from her eyes. Her fear was confirmed when he looked out at the court and said, "If you'll excuse us for a moment."

The king stood and gently escorted Abigail into a side

chamber. He shut the door behind him and turned the lock in place.

She took a step back. "Are you going to kill me too if I talk back?" Tears streamed down her face.

"Abby, please don't cry." The king moved closer and wiped the dampness from her cheeks. "You'll make your face all red."

"Why are you doing this? You humiliated me in front of my family. Now you're killing a man for not liking your choice in slave? Nobody should have to die for me!"

The king seemed more unstable by the minute, just another shade, another flavor, of evil, no better than his gypsy-killing father. She tried not to think about his hands on her the night before, or just moments ago in court. She couldn't let herself react sexually to such a man.

"I didn't realize your family would have a problem, but I understand your shyness better now. You will get over it. I won't be more lenient just because you were raised in a repressed environment. That nonsense will end," he said. "As for Mark, he has been a thorn in my side for months. I've been waiting for the right moment to send him to his maker. Too many people inside the walls of this castle have taken my mercy for weakness. I didn't realize when I took the throne that I was in another war, one with my own people. I had hoped someone would lash out, and I'm glad it was Mark. An execution sends the message more clearly. It will keep you safe. I don't want anyone else breaking my toy."

Abigail cringed at that last part, but then he pulled her close to him and held her, gently stroking her back. It confirmed yet another cultural difference between them. To her *my toy* seemed demeaning and cruel, but he'd obviously meant it as an endearment.

"You'll get used to our ways. You'll even come to enjoy them." He held her quietly for another minute. "Are you finished with the tears, now?"

"Yes, Master." It was all she could say. He didn't owe her an explanation for his actions. The fact that he'd given her one must count for something.

"Good. We need to get back."

Although she didn't like it, there was a sense of logic to his stance. After all, even she had let her guard down before he'd spanked her the previous night. It was too easy to forget his power if he didn't display and enforce it. He had to protect his position and wanted to protect his property as well. For that, she felt she should be grateful, or at the very least, not surly.

If anyone in the kingdom thought going against his choice in a slave was okay, it could put her life in danger.

When they returned, the king didn't direct her to kneel on the cushion, but to lie down on the chaise.

Abigail lay on the king's lap as he greeted foreign guests who'd traveled for the festival. They would be staying in the guest wing. As they exchanged pleasantries, the king pulled the pins from her hair to let it fall freely around her shoulders. She let out a shaky breath. Although she'd been mentally preparing herself for what came next, she still let out a shocked little whimper when he spread her thighs and began to rub between her legs. She shuddered against his hand, surprised by how ready her body was for his touch even surrounded by a roomful of voyeurs.

The panties underneath the strands of beads and jewels had been made with the king's interests in mind. It wasn't a solid piece of cloth, but two pieces that overlapped and could be easily pulled aside. The king slipped a finger between her nether lips, possessively stroking her as he spoke to one of the guests.

Her face heated at being on display, even as she felt warmth and wetness growing between her thighs. She stifled a moan, but the king noticed.

"Don't hold back, Abby. I want to hear your pleasure. I want everyone to hear it. You will surrender to me whenever and however I demand." Despite his proclamation, he'd issued his directions in a low, gravelly whisper.

She bit her lip and looked up. "Please," she said, knowing she was far from ready for something like this. She was still overwhelmed by all the changes. "You know I can't ... "

"Remember what happened last night when you told me that?"

It was all she needed to hear. Being spanked bare-assed in front of the nobles, guards, and guests of the castle would be far worse than moaning for them. She had to remember how others saw things if she wanted to spare herself maximum humiliation. They wouldn't care or be shocked or appalled by witnessing a sexual display.

The king returned his attention to his guest who was obviously a first-time visitor to Himeros, because, while the man looked painfully aroused, he also looked quite shocked with the casual way Abigail was being touched in open court. The king didn't seem to notice, or if he did, he was so used to these reactions from strangers that he paid it no mind other than mild amusement at the prudery of other kingdoms.

"As you can see, I don't have a full harem. I only have Abigail. However, I'm sure one of the young women origi-nally trained for my harem would be happy to serve their king by entertaining you during your stay. I understand they give wonderful erotic massages, and sonnets have been written about their oral skills."

The man's eyes lit as the king motioned to one of the guards. A side door opened and in came several beautiful, blonde women, their skin so pale it was almost translucent. They'd obviously never seen sunlight for more than a few minutes at a time, always kept covered and in the shade to preserve their milky-white complexions.

Abigail looked away from the jealousy and distaste in their eyes. They weren't wearing the same clothes as she was. Her garments were only for those the king had personally chosen for his harem. Their clothing was beautiful and no less revealing of their curves, but there were no jewels or beads in sight, only expensive fabric with intricate embroidery and some ribbons.

The guest, though obviously desiring the understudy harem, seemed skeptical. Though he didn't dare say it, Abigail could guess his hesitation was because he wondered what was wrong with them if the king had rejected them. Her master seemed to sense the same question.

"I have...more exotic tastes," the king said. During the conversation he'd continued to stroke Abigail, her orgasm catching her by surprise. She couldn't stop the moan that issued from her mouth. Her cheeks flushed at the stunned expression on the stranger's face, and she looked away from him.

"You're free to select someone now," the king said. "I'm sure you're quite worked up from the show."

The man moved in a daze toward the blonde women and picked one from the line. She gave him a fake smile and made a little bow, then exited out the back door with him. No doubt, they were going to his room to test the sonnet theory.

As the next guest stepped forward, the king removed Abigail's top so he could fondle her bare breasts. The man was appreciative of the view but showed no shock as he watched her nipples harden in response to the groping.

"Sir Frederick," the king said, "It's wonderful to see you again. Couldn't stay away?"

Fredrick shook his head. He looked to be around thirty and was nearly as handsome as the king. He bowed. "It's good of you to have me here, Your Majesty. It's always a breath of fresh air to be in Himeros where the women aren't so uptight. It's a mystery to me why men in other lands have worked so hard to suppress female sexuality when they could be displaying it." His gaze went to Abigail, drinking her in, almost physically violating her with only a look. "She's exquisite," he said. "I'm jealous."

The king laughed and waved him off. Frederick crooked a finger at a woman from the line. She grinned at him as if they had a history, and maybe they did. Abigail was surprised when he didn't take her out of the court, but instead moved to the far wall to one of many ornate couches. The woman didn't seem to mind, uninhibitedly removing her clothing and kneeling at his feet. He sat on the couch and undid his pants, freeing his impressive cock. The woman took him into her mouth without hesitation, as if it was the best thing she'd ever had between her lips.

Abigail watched in twisted fascination as the woman bobbed up and down on the man's member. He glanced up and held Abby's eyes with a knowing smirk until she looked away.

The king was right: Abigail may as well have been a virgin for all her naiveté about the debauchery of court. The pattern repeated itself over the next hour or so. The king greeted guests, and they each picked a woman to entertain them during their stay. Some retired to their guest room, while others stayed and fondled and fucked in the open, slowly turning the proceedings into a mini-orgy as guests swapped women or put them together to watch them pleasure each other for everyone's amusement. Abigail had known this went on at court, but seeing it or being a part of it was something quite different.

She should have felt more shame, but the comfort and acceptance of everyone in attendance made it seem normal and less tawdry. Titillating and exciting, but not wrong.

When the guests had been greeted and everyone was settled and involved in their own activities, the smell of sex growing stronger in the air by the minute, the king stood and moved to the other side of the chaise.

"Get on your hands and knees." His voice was strained, barely above a low growl. It wasn't just the guests and nobles whose excitement had grown higher as they'd watched Abigail writhe against the king's hand. He'd had to wait until the formalities were past before he could lose himself inside her.

She didn't hesitate, afraid to keep the king waiting for even another second. In record time, he'd divested himself of his clothing, perfectly comfortable and content to display his own nudity. He took the belt and panties off her, careful not to tear them. She'd grown so sensitive as he'd rubbed and teased her, his fingers dancing along the wet folds of her most private parts, that she groaned with relief when she was finally impaled on him.

As the king used her, Sir Frederick approached, wearing nothing but a cocky smirk.

"May I touch her?"

The king must have nodded because a second later, Frederick squeezed and stroked her breasts. His hands slid over her thighs and belly and hips as if she were a side of meat he might purchase for his table. Then he stroked his cock a few inches from her face.

"Frederick is an old and dear friend and ally," the king said. "Open your mouth for him, Abby. Let him get inside you."

She hesitated, but then opened and allowed the stranger to slide into the warmth of her mouth, reveling in her own degradation and the hedonism that had taken them all like a demonic possession.

"She's shy. I didn't know such a thing existed in Himeros," Frederick commented, sounding genuinely surprised.

"She is a rare flower, indeed," the king said. "I'll be almost sad when she's jaded to all of this. Watching her reactions to each new stimulus pleases me very much."

Abigail still felt uncomfortable, but she couldn't deny a dark part of her was aroused by the sexual attention. Becoming their vessel and toy loosened the tension within her. The many long years of worrying constantly about food and shelter and feeling unwell melted away, replaced with only a single concern at the forefront of her mind: pleasing the king and whomever he shared her with.

"May I instruct her?" Frederick asked.

"Be my guest."

Frederick moved his hand to her cheek, petting her as if she were a farm animal he was coaxing to give milk. "Relax your jaw, sweetheart."

When she did, he said, "Good girl. Now I'm going to move in and out of you. I want you to lick and suck it for me."

The arousal pulsed harder between Abigail's legs as she

followed the demeaning instructions. The king had been taking his time fucking her, patiently moving in and out, waking all of her nerve endings with a tantalizing slowness. Meanwhile, Frederick spoke soothing nonsense as he stroked her hair and fucked her mouth.

When he began to move faster, so did the king. Abigail felt as though she were falling off a cliff with nothing holding her up but these two powerful men. She held on tight as both of them rode her, coming inside her in tandem. Her walls contracted around the king as she came, and he groaned out the last of his release.

Both of the men eased out of her and Frederick laughed. "Yes, I am definitely jealous."

The king picked up a boneless and sated Abigail and carried her to his chambers where she was allowed a much-deserved nap.

WITH EACH DAY THAT PASSED, NIALL FOUND HIMSELF MORE pleased with his acquisition. Despite her shyness and frequent blushing, she never failed to comply with what he demanded of her. He'd upgraded to using toys in court. He derived great amusement, stuffing her with large phalluses, growing hard as she fucked herself on them in front of their guests

He enjoyed tying her spread-eagled to a large oak table and allowing members of court to fondle her as long as they wanted. It aroused him to watch her writhe under the hands of another—many others.

But aside from his friend, Frederick, he didn't allow any of them to fuck her. Even Frederick was only allowed use of her mouth. Niall enjoyed binding her naked body with increasingly intricate knotwork. He'd instructed the servants to keep her shaved bare so nothing would be hidden from the gaze of the court. He saw her shyness as a challenge to expose her body more fully to increasing numbers of strangers. Her embarrassment and discomfort were an aphrodisiac.

The festival was held outdoors. Being under the open sky tended to bring out a darker, more primal side in most attendants. Each day of the feast, Abigail's family had been invited only for the early portion, before things got wild. Then they were dismissed, along with the children so the adults could play.

Niall was disappointed Abby's father seemed no closer to accepting anything that had transpired. He'd chosen to stay in the home the king had given him rather than venture out to the festival. At least Abby's mother and siblings had attended the dinners.

On the final night of the festival, Niall had Abby dressed in a dazzling gold slave garment that made her look even more exotic than usual.

"You look like an angel," her youngest sister proclaimed. "I want to be just like you when I grow up."

A darkness swept over the mother's features as she looked at the king. As if Niall would stoop so low as to take his slave's sister when she came of age.

"Not going to happen," he said. Abby's mother seemed moderately appeased.

Bells rang out over loudspeakers, signaling the need to clear out children and those who didn't wish to participate in the orgy and ceremony. Torches were lit and the tone of the music shifted from an upbeat tune to a slow and sensuous drumbeat with serpentine sounds that drifted and coiled around the banquet tables along with the smoke of hundreds of candles.

Abigail hugged her mother and siblings, and they departed to their house. Then the wine and harder liquor flowed freely. As the music got slow and sensual, the frenetic energy of the remaining guests grew wilder, more primal.

Niall observed the nervous tension in his slave. She seemed to sense the flavor of things shifting, not just for this portion of the night, but for the end of the festival. As if everything were more desperate and less inhibited.

Abby looked on in horror at the depravity that had been kicked to a new level. Over at one table, two men held a woman's thighs open while they coaxed a dog to lick between her legs. She screamed, "No, please, stop," but it was clearly an act, because she was giggling and pressing her mound harder against the dog's tongue, already approaching her orgasm. Then the men started pouring wine over her breasts and sucking it off, teasing her with threats of even worse things they had in store for her later.

"Are you all right, Abigail?" Niall asked as he came closer and wrapped his arms around her. Despite not wanting to coddle her, he was concerned by how she'd take some of the more extreme behaviors.

"Aren't you going to stop that?" She pointed at the woman with the men and dog.

"Why? No one is in any danger. The dog isn't being forced. No one is being hurt."

"It's just so ... gross."

He shrugged, long past too jaded to care about the introduction of animals to the evening's festivities. It was her first formal orgy; she'd adjust eventually. A few of the foreign guests on their first trip to Himeros would surely go back to report on what barbaric demons they all were, even though it was only one small trio engaging in the activity. People loved to blow things out of proportion.

"What about that?" Abigail pointed to where a woman had been tied down and was being struck with a riding crop.

"Beg to be fucked with it, little slut," the man with the crop snarled.

"Please, Sir, stop," she whimpered. "I-I don't want to."

"Wrong answer." He struck her again, laying a sharp red line across her bare ass. "Try again."

She mewled and strained against her bonds. "Please, Sir, fuck me with it."

He turned the riding crop so that the long, thick handle was poised at her entrance, but then he stopped and moved in front of her, holding the crop at her mouth. "It needs lube."

She wet it with her saliva, then he moved back behind her and pushed it into her ass.

The woman let out a howl. "Please..."

"I'm sorry, my dear. You disobeyed me. It would have been your cunt if you'd asked sweetly the first time. You could be coming against the crop handle right now if you'd been more pleasing."

Niall chuckled at the scene and shook his head. "I know both of them, Abby. It might not appear that way, but believe me, they are both completely into it. It's just a game they play."

"A-are you into it, Master?" she asked.

The tremulous tone of her voice made him hard. "Watching or doing?" he asked.

"D-doing."

"Yes, it pleases me, and eventually you'll be in her position, so when I tell you to beg for something, you'd better do it quickly because I know all his tricks."

Niall watched as she processed that, then he stepped behind her and cupped her mound. It was warm, her wetness already slipping through the gap in the fabric of her panties. When he pressed his fingers against her, he could feel the throbbing pulse as her blood rushed past. However scared she might be by all of it, the idea aroused her, too, though he doubted she'd admit it unless he ordered her to.

"Are you ready to be put on the stage?"

Her breathing and manner changed to a heady mixture of arousal and fear. "Yes, Master," she whispered.

He knew it was a lie, but let it go. Having just witnessed the couple with the riding crop, she seemed ill-prepared to give even the impression of non-compliance, likely for fear he might do something similar to her up on the well-lit stage.

The king took her hand and led her up the steps. A sturdy oak table with straps attached stood on one end of the platform. On the other end was a gilded bench that had been bolted to the floor with a thick phallus attached. He nudged Abigail closer to it and slipped her top off, followed by the belt and panties. The bracelets, anklets, and diamond and gold chain around her waist were left on. Her hair fell free down her back in waves.

The music changed, and the drumbeats got stronger and deeper, so hard and loud that they would thump through the body of each person in attendance, bringing them more fully into the proceedings. They were mesmerized by the sight of her. If they'd had any hatred for her ancestry, it had fizzled in the heat of orgasm and alcohol.

Niall stood behind his slave, gripping the front of her

tasting her. The guards strapped her down on the table, spread-eagled, and one by one his subjects came up onto the platform to lick between her legs. Some took a small taste, others lingered longer, seeking a deeper connection to honor the gods and to wring more pleasure from her body.

Abigail writhed and twisted under each tongue. She bucked as some dipped inside her, not content to lick her outer folds. Others fingered her pussy to draw more wetness out for the enjoyment of those who came after them. He didn't stand in the way of any subject seeking to share in the ritual.

When everyone had tasted her, Niall motioned for Frederick, who bounded up the stairs two at a time.

"Your Majesty?"

"Stay with her. But no penetration except her mouth," Niall said. He wanted to be sure she wasn't left alone and vulnerable.

"You ruin all my fun," came the reply.

"I mean it."

Frederick mock-bowed and said: "Yes, Your Majesty."

Niall just shook his head and stepped down from the stage. When he turned around, Abby was still tied down, sucking his friend.

He wanted to take a quick look around and make sure everything was as it should be now that the ritual was over. He had the party well-guarded but he still liked to keep an eye on things. It was a deeply imprinted instinct from times of war when he'd had to remain on constant alert.

On the final leg of his patrol, he rounded a corner to find Yvette, one of the girls who'd been trained for his harem. She was naked and looked to be lying in wait for someone. She'd already been well and thoroughly used, judging from the flush of her cheeks, her swollen lips, and the wetness running down her thighs, likely a mixture of her own moisture and the spendings of the many men she'd serviced tonight.

"Your Majesty," she said, dropping to her knees and crawling closer. She reached up for him, as if to initiate a sexual act she hadn't been given permission for.

Oh. She'd been lying in wait for him. Wonderful.

"Yvette," he said, with a slight nod and a simultaneous step back.

Her eyes glinted, and for a moment she forgot her place and the supreme power the king held over her very life. "Why aren't we good enough for you? We've been trained. We know how to please you. We don't have to be instructed on anything. So what the hell is wrong with us?"

Niall sighed. "You want to know what's wrong with you? You're playing a game. You and every other woman in the harem. You know how to manipulate a man to get what you want. He may think he owns you, but you own him. There is power and money in your eyes. You dream of being the mother to the future king and all the things you could get me to buy for you and give you and all the ways I could indulge you. You have no real need or desire to serve. You just want to take. That's why you aren't good enough."

The anger sparked brighter. "It should have been me on that stage. You think your precious Abigail is more worthy? You think she's any less *manipulative* than us? How else would a poor gypsy end up in the king's bed with all this finery around her? You're naïve if you don't see she's no different from me. She's a bigger con artist than I'll ever be."

"Careful how you speak to me. Abigail is the real thing." Wasn't she? Of course she was, but the seed, however untrustworthy the source, had been planted.

Yvette stood as gracefully as possible under the circumstances and brushed past him. She paused when she reached the end of the wall and turned back to the king. "But how would you really know?"

As she made her exit, he gripped her hard around the arm.

"Ow! You're hurting me."

"Be glad that's all I'm doing." Niall escorted her to the edge of the grounds and handed her off to one of the guards. "Yvette is to be banned from castle grounds. Send her back to her family."

She struggled, trying to pull away. "No, please, Master. Don't send me back home. It will shame the family. It's bad enough you won't use me."

"Do *not* ever call me that. It's not your right." He turned to the guard. "Get her out of here. I don't want her near me or Abigail again."

As Niall walked back through the throng of revelers, he thought about what Yvette had said. She was wrong. Of course she was wrong. His Abby wasn't like that. She hadn't chosen any of this. It wasn't as if she'd positioned herself right in front of him. Or had she?

He knew Yvette was jealous. But that didn't mean the woman couldn't be right. He'd watched so carefully for signs of those around him who might try to undermine his reign.

Could Abigail have manipulated the whole thing from the beginning? Wasn't it at least possible? Why else would she have taken such a dangerous chance to steal bread from the castle, of all places? And why end up conveniently right outside his door during her escape attempt? His stomach turned at what he was considering. He didn't want to believe it was possible, but anything was possible. Greater men had been brought down by beautiful and seemingly helpless women.

IN ONLY A FEW WEEKS, ABIGAIL HAD ADJUSTED TO HER POSITION in the kingdom. Her family had been invited to dinner several times. Her father refused the invitations, of course. It irritated her because he seemed happy enough to live in the house the king had given him after his initial angry outburst.

Niall had been nothing but polite and proper during dinners with her family, only turning the evening sexual when they were a safe distance from the castle. Her brothers and sisters didn't seem to fully understand her position with the king, and her mother appeared to be trying to forget it, but seeing how healthy and happy Abigail looked had seemed to quiet the woman's inner demons.

There was only one thing that kept everything from being perfect. The king was pulling away from her. It had started the final night of the festival. She'd wanted to ask what she'd done wrong, but she was afraid to broach the subject and appear too aggressive. She didn't want to displease him further.

Her loneliness grew as she became more attached and dependent on him and the necessities he provided her, while he became increasingly detached and distracted. Maybe he was just growing bored with her.

He was the first king in recent history to have a single slave, rejecting an official harem and only keeping those girls around to entertain guests. Did he want a harem? If he wanted one, why didn't he just start one? He was the king. He didn't need Abigail's permission. She didn't know how she would feel if he took more women and she got pushed to the side. She hoped she'd remain special since she'd been the first, but with their growing distance, it seemed unlikely he'd keep her at all.

The door opened and two servant girls entered. "The king wants you prepared for him and brought to court at once." There was an edge of anxiety in the voice of the woman who'd spoken.

The servants rushed her through a bath, the fragrant oils haphazardly thrown into the water. There was no time for a long, languid soak.

"He wants you in this one," the other girl said, holding up a red slave garment. The red would be striking and dramatic against Abigail's black hair. It was stupid to think about such vain things when obviously something was about to happen. She didn't make a fuss when they hauled her out of the tub and toweled her off.

Her eyes looked glassy and unfocused in the full-length mirror as they helped her into the top and panties and belt. Next came the anklets and bracelets, and the chain that went around her belly. The previous night, her nails had been painted a scarlet red. She looked down at her bare feet and wondered if Niall had seen her nails and chosen this garment to match. If he had, it gave her hope he hadn't completely lost interest—if he could notice small details like what color her nails had been painted.

"Quickly," one of them said, running a brush through Abigail's hair and guiding her out of the king's chambers. They hadn't lost the frenetic energy since they'd interrupted her breakfast. Things were never like this when the servants came. It made Abigail worry even more that she'd inadvertently done something to displease the king.

Though she'd seen him make righteous and just decisions in the several weeks she'd been in his care, she'd also seen the swift punishment he delivered to anybody who stepped out of line even a little. He'd become increasingly paranoid about how his subjects were reacting to him, thinking someone would wish to overthrow him if he showed the slightest hint of weakness. She could tell he felt pressure to become someone he wasn't to secure his throne. Or someone she hoped he wasn't.

But the more he behaved like his father, the more Abigail cringed inwardly. If he made the complete metamorphosis, he'd look at her one day, see her dark skin and gypsy features and do something about it. Maybe that day had already arrived.

Abigail took a deep breath as she descended the stairs. Two guards nodded and opened the door for her. She glided in, feeling weirdly self-conscious in front of everyone at court, though none of her clothing had come off yet and she was weeks past embarrassment over her own nudity. She moved to her cushion by the king's feet to await his orders, but he shook his head.

"No. Stand right there. You're here on official business today."

Business? His gray eyes had gone a harsh slate, like tar-blackened snow in the winter.

"Master?"

"Tell me, Abigail ... why are you here with me?"

"I beg your pardon?"

"Why are you here? It's a simple enough question. All I require is a simple answer."

"I'm here at your pleasure because you chose to spare me from the guard that wanted to harm me."

"Are you?" His gaze held suspicion and a touch of cold malice. A chill went down her spine at that shrewd look being directed at her. She'd seen it leveled at criminals and the stray noble who'd shown hints of disloyalty, but never at her. Though he'd grown more detached, he hadn't seemed angry before now.

The king continued, "So you have no designs on power or wealth or being mother to the future king? This wasn't some plot all along to get into my bed?"

"I ... Master, I don't know where this is coming from. I'm here because of your choice to keep me. Though I'm deeply grateful, I didn't ask for anything you've given me, nor have I held any expectations for the future."

"Really? We'll see. Come here."

She took the few steps to close the gap between them with a slowness that surprised even her. It had been foolish to forget what she was. How would it ever work between a king of Himeros and a gypsy? It couldn't. Perhaps pressure had been put on him from outside forces. Or maybe he'd come to his senses on his own. Or this had been his plan all along. Why not? She'd attempted to steal from him. The only way he could return the favor is if she had something worth taking.

"Please, Master. I don't know what I did. Have I not pleased you? Have I ever asked for a single thing or shown any ingratitude toward you?"

In response he gripped her wrist and pulled her onto his lap. He grabbed her breast and squeezed, roughly. "Do you mean to tell me you'd be happy as nothing but my common whore? Without the finery? Would you be happy if I shared you with everyone without discrimination to use you in any degrading way they saw fit?"

No, she wouldn't be happy that way, and he knew it. "I'd be anything you wanted me to be," she said, barely above a whisper, still not believing any of this was happening and becoming increasingly frightened for her life. At the rate the king was going, a noose around her neck didn't sound outside the realm of the possible.

He released her breast, his hand going around her neck as if he'd read her mind.

"John," he barked.

"Yes, Your Majesty?" the guard said from the back of the room.

"How would you like to fuck my gypsy?"

Murmurs rose around her, a stifling and oppressive din of noise. She heard John's heavy boots as he came up behind her. He was the king's most favored guard and the best.

He'd looked at her before with clear desire. She wouldn't have minded being sent to his bed if the king had commanded it. He was level-headed and honorable and good-looking and strong. But like this? The king wasn't rewarding John; he was trying to shame her.

"Why are you doing this?" Abigail said, barely above a choked whisper. She was too afraid to speak louder, afraid she'd enrage him by talking back loud enough for their audience to hear.

"I'm going to make you an offer," the king said. "You have two choices. You can leave the castle and go live with your family in the house I've provided them, or you can submit to my head guard, right here, right now."

She glanced over at John, who watched her intensely. She couldn't tell what he was thinking. Whenever she looked at the guard the only words she could think to describe him were: blank slate. Even when he seemed intense, she couldn't begin to fathom what specific thoughts lay behind his intensity.

Today was no different. She couldn't tell right now if he wanted to fuck her, if he was disgusted by all this, if he pitied her. She hoped he didn't pity her. Spreading her legs for John, even under these circumstances, wasn't something she'd class as a punishment. As long as he didn't hurt her. But she didn't think he would, not unless the king commanded him to.

"All right," she said. "If that's what you want."

She moved in a daze to the chaise lounge that she normally reclined on next to the king, John following behind her. She heard the clinking of his belt as he unbuckled it, and she sucked in a breath, aroused in spite of everything.

"Wait," Niall said.

Abigail looked over at him, wondering if he'd been bluffing the whole time, and if so, what possible reason he could have for it. She still didn't understand why he was giving her these strange choices: go live with her family or have sex with his guard.

Even with the king's distance of late, she didn't want to sleep in a bed without him. Whatever test this was—if it was a test and not just delayed gypsy hatred—she would pass it. She'd do whatever it took to prove she wasn't using him. All she'd ever done was serve and obey him. It's all she ever wanted to do.

"Whip her first. Otherwise she might like it too much."

Cold terror shot through her at the command. The king had never whipped her nor had her whipped. The most she'd experienced at his hand was the occasional spanking, but even that was rare. She'd been so grateful to him for the life he'd given her that she'd been utterly devoted. Punishments were small and for trifling missteps. Nothing more.

This seemed like more.

Abigail heard the hesitation in the change of the guard's breathing. She knew he didn't want to hurt her. As loyal as John was, at least he could see she meant no one any harm. If he wouldn't do it, what then? She silently prayed John would obey the request because she feared Niall would only call upon another guard, one that was less kind if he didn't.

"Your Majesty, I ... "

"Yes, John?" the king said mildly, daring him to challenge a command at court. Niall turned to Abigail. "Abby, I'll give you another chance. You don't have to go through any of this. I will pardon you for your manipulation and will allow you to live in luxury with your family. All you have to do is accept my pardon."

Abigail stubbornly shook her head, the tears gathering behind her eyes, both because of Niall's betrayal as well as fear of the pain that was coming. She wanted to speak with him privately, away from all these people. He'd turned this into a show, and now too much was at stake for him to back down. He wouldn't retreat on her say-so. However he'd gotten it into his head that she was manipulating him, it was there now, firmly stuck. It was why he'd been pulling away: he didn't trust her.

She was playing a fool's game. If the king didn't trust you, the wisest thing to do was take the out he gave you. By this point, the longer she insisted on staying near him the greater the odds her life would be forfeit by the end.

"Very well," the king said, "but I'm not a monster. You can stop this at any time if you wish to go stay with your family. It's not an heir to the throne or a position in court, but it's still money and food and shelter. I can't fault you for wanting any of that. Anyone would. To stop this, all you have to do is beg for mercy, and I'll give it to you."

The room had gone completely silent save for the ominous sound of the sturdy oak table being rolled out. John and another guard tied her down on her stomach so she couldn't pull away, then the other guard released the latch on her top and let it fall open, exposing her back.

"You'll break," the king said. "This pain will be pointless in the end. Beg mercy now and spare yourself the pain and indignity."

Abigail shook her head. She felt numb, some part of her convinced none of this was really happening. People were talking in the background, but it all sounded like it was coming from very far away. She looked up at the king in time to see him nod at John.

The whip came down, causing a stinging lick of fire to trail down her back. She jerked hard against her bonds. The pain was so quick and brutal that it felt as if she'd been pulled momentarily out of her body, then shoved back in again. She tried to brace herself for the next blow, but having felt the pain of the first strike, it was useless. The second lash was just as hard and frightening as the first and just as unexpected in its intensity.

Each time the whip struck her flesh, Abigail cried out, but she didn't beg or plead. She didn't form any words that might indicate she'd take the king's insane offer. Although his behavior toward her was abysmal, it still couldn't kill the gratitude she felt for all he'd given her.

"Ready for mercy yet?" the king taunted.

"No, Master." The words sounded weaker than they did in her head. Somehow the defiant tone hadn't translated when she'd said it aloud.

The whip came down again and again and she wondered when it would stop, if it would ever stop. She wondered if the king would let John whip her to death if she didn't cave. She felt like a witch in an inquisition. *Confess! Confess! Confess, and I'll pardon you.* But she hadn't done anything to confess, and she wouldn't dishonor her name with a lie to soothe the troubled king.

As the whip struck her again, she glanced up in time to see Niall flinch.

Abigail met his gaze as she let out another cry. If he was going to do this to her, she'd make him truly see what he was doing. The king's eyes were haunted, but he quickly forced the expression off his face. She must be bleeding by now. The pain had numbed out a little, and that scared her even more, almost enough to beg.

"Stop," he said. "She's had enough."

The tears fell harder, more relief than anything. She rested her cheek against the table as she listened to the whip being rolled back into a coil and returned to the guard's belt. Then the footsteps started to recede.

"Aren't you forgetting something, John?" the king said.

Niall had composed himself and was now set on giving the court a show: a show of what happened to a woman who thought to manipulate him to get her way. The would-be harem was in attendance, one or two of them looking smug, but most of them terrified. Abigail bet none of them envied her any longer.

"Will you beg mercy now, Abby?" the king asked. No one else could detect it, but she knew him well enough to hear the edge of emotion in his voice, the tiny bit of pleading that she would ask for his mercy so it could all stop.

"No, Master. I don't wish to go live with my family. I want to stay with you, and I'll do whatever it takes to prove that."

Niall shook his head. "This won't end like you imagine. I've made up my mind."

As much as she should hate the king and want to rip out his organs right now, she didn't. She pitied him. He'd inherited a kingdom with subjects who only respected kings they could fear, because they didn't know any better way. So the cycle of abuse continued. And now she was caught in the middle of it, more a victim of circumstance than of Niall.

Abigail closed her eyes while John fucked her, her body limp and loose and unresisting as he entered her over and over. She'd become the king's receptive vessel, gratefully accepting any and all penetration, and this was no different.

Niall may have wanted to break her, to be proven right, that no one could make a fool of him, but he was the broken one. She'd seen it on his face. Strangely, the more he did to her, the stronger she became, the less she allowed it to touch her, and the more she knew it hurt him.

"If you like all this so much, perhaps you should give us a nice, long orgasm," Niall said. "Maybe I'll have you whipped again if you don't."

It was the final nail in the coffin meant to undo her, but he'd already twisted her mind so deeply and so far that even the perverse suggestion had a twitch starting between her legs, followed by a low throb that built stronger the longer the guard rode her.

Suddenly the idea of the court finally shocked by watching something sexual made her fight to have the orgasm the king had suggested, just for spite. She'd faced greater hardships than this just getting by day to day before Niall had entered her life. She'd die before she gave him the satisfaction of breaking her for crimes she'd never committed against him.

The guard seemed shocked when her orgasm rippled through her and she let out a low, satisfied moan. While others in the court might think she'd faked it, John must have felt the pulses as her cunt gripped him hard, as if she were the aggressor. The guard, however, hadn't found his own completion. He pulled out of her without finishing.

"Shameless slut," Niall said, but there was no malice in the pronouncement, only pride.

She looked up at him. "Like you trained me to be."

A small smile played at the corner of his mouth, but then it was gone, not even leaving the ghost of amusement behind. She'd thought in that small moment that it was over, that he'd come to his senses. He'd never apologize to her. He was the king. Kings didn't apologize; they couldn't afford to. But she didn't require his apology. It was only important that he knew she'd never betrayed him nor tried to hurt him. As long as things went back somehow to the way they'd been before the festival she'd forgive him anything.

But it wasn't to be. "Strip her of her finery and take her to the dungeon," he said. "If she won't take the gifts and pardon I offer her, then she'll be treated like a criminal."

Could this really be happening? Was he really abandoning her like this? Surely his wrath and ego had been appeased. It didn't seem possible it was ending this way.

Rather than drag her roughly off, John untied her and carried her to the dungeon. He stripped her only once she was out of sight of others. By that point she was crying harder than she had when he'd whipped her.

"Are you hungry?" he asked, once he had her in a cell. It

was damp and too cold, the kind of place she could easily imagine dying in.

"Not yet," Abigail said. "I had a big breakfast." She knew her attempt at bravery was falling flat.

"That's the last of that, I'm afraid. I don't know what you did to piss him off, but I've never seen him like this. Even in battle he never behaved this way."

"I didn't do anything. He's wrong."

"Kings can't be wrong," John replied.

Maybe Niall couldn't have even been wrong in private if it had only been the two of them. She should hate him. She knew it would be the normal reaction, but she couldn't help feeling hurt for him. How must it feel to let no one in, ever? To not be able to? Even through her darkest times, she'd had her family to lean on and confide in, at least until she'd become the king's slave. Now she had no one.

When her father discovered her fall from grace, she wondered if he'd think it was what she deserved for being such a whore, that this was what came of selling yourself, even though she'd done no such thing. Niall had never given her any indication her wishes would have any bearing on his choice to keep her. Given the circumstances, he'd shown her mercy. Until today.

There was a leak somewhere off in the distance, a maddening *drip, drip, drip*. How would she exist with that as her life's background track? She allowed her fingers to trail over a cold, damp algae growing on the stone wall. She'd catch her death here.

Abigail curled into a ball on the dirt floor. She shivered in the draft without clothing or blankets, her own body the only thing she could try to derive warmth from. Somehow, in spite of the conditions, she drifted into an exhausted sleep.

She jumped suddenly at the feel of strong hands on her back. Warm water sluiced down, causing pain as it flowed over tender flesh. Her eyes drifted open as memories slowly seeped through the fog of her awareness. She twisted her body, expecting to discover the king tending to her wounds, but it was a dungeon guard.

"Why...?"

"I'm just following orders," the stranger said, drying her with a clean towel. He worked quickly and carefully as he applied bandages to her back.

She tried unsuccessfully not to cry. How stupid to think it was the king. Why would the king ever lower himself to entering the dungeon? The idea that he would sit in this filth and actually clean and dress her wounds was wishful thinking of the highest order. She had to let that life go, no matter how difficult it was.

When the guard finished tending to her, he gathered the supplies and started to leave. He paused at the door. "I've brought you food and blankets, just over there in the corner." He pointed.

She hadn't noticed them in the dim lighting. "Thank you." The food was only bread and water, but at least it was fresh on both counts. She'd had worse.

A few days passed like this, and Abigail sank further into hopelessness. The only small reprieve was when a guard came—a different one each time—to change her bandages and bathe her. Each time, she closed her eyes and imagined it was the king.

Why couldn't he have just executed her? Keeping her in a dark little cell forever was heartless. There was no life or hope to look forward to. No hope of freedom or ever seeing Niall again.

She startled when heavy footsteps moved toward her, expecting another guard. But it was the king who unlocked the door and stepped inside. Instinctively she moved toward him, kneeling at his feet, her cheek resting against his boot. She didn't know why he'd come, but she had to be close to him.

"Well, Abby, are you ready to admit it now?"

She wanted to tell him anything he wanted to hear, but she couldn't bring herself to say the lie that would free her. Her honor was all she had left. "I have nothing to admit, Master."

He sighed. "This is your final chance. You can go quietly now to live with your family, or you can stay in the dungeon for the rest of your life. I won't offer you any more opportunities. Surely you've had time to think this through."

"My answer is still the same." She wouldn't admit defeat now. She wouldn't give him the satisfaction of pretending she'd ever been anything but his loyal slave. If she was to die down here, then she would. If he was too stubborn to admit he was wrong, then her death would be on his hands.

"Very well, if that's your answer."

"It is."

She expected him to turn and leave her there to rot, but he scooped her up and carried her, wrapped in the dirty blankets, back upstairs. He deposited her gently on the tile of his bathroom and turned on the water for the bath. He was silent as he began to drop the rose petals and pour in the fragrant oils.

"Go. Shower the dirt off," he said, pointing as if time had rewound itself and it was their first night together. Only this time, bizarrely, she didn't fear him or what he might do to her, even though he'd given her plenty of valid reasons to.

She went to the shower. The wounds on her back were still tender, though they'd closed now and were healing. She'd been healthy enough at the time of the whipping that her body had mended itself even on the lower quality food in her cell.

She breathed in the scent of the delicate lavender and oat soap as she scrubbed off the grime from the dungeon, hardly believing this could be real. She took the towel from the peg and dried off, then moved tentatively toward the tub.

"Abigail..." The king's voice was threaded with more emotion than she'd ever heard from him.

"Yes, Master?"

He seemed as if he were preparing to say something important, but instead he said, "Get in the tub."

She got in and leaned back, closing her eyes. A little moan left her as she sank into the water, letting the soothing warmth take the remaining pain from the whip marks.

"How can you relax like that?" he asked after a minute. "How can you be anything but terrified of me after what I did?"

She opened her eyes, shocked to find tears rolling down his cheeks. "Am I going back to the dungeon?"

"No. Never," he said fiercely.

"So you believe me? You know I didn't set this up?"

He nodded, his arms crossed over his chest. "It was a test. I had myself half convinced you'd scammed me, that you were making a mockery of me, maybe getting some strange revenge for my father's behavior. But I let it get out of control. I'd expected you'd beg for mercy—even if you were innocent —and that I'd give you a slap on the wrist and take you back after a time. But when you didn't break, with all those witnesses..."

"Did you kill them?" Abigail asked, her voice oddly light.

"God, no! What kind of monster..."

"I was kidding." It was the first time they'd spoken like this. Real. Honest. A slight edge of disrespect. She didn't know where it came from, but she wanted to lighten things, let him know she was really okay.

"How can you be so casual about this? How can you even want to belong to me after this? I shamed you and violated your trust." His features were open. He was finally letting her in. Being let into his confidence was worth all that had transpired, but she knew he'd never see it that way.

"I was here at your pleasure. I was in the dungeon at your pleasure. You're the king, and you can do what you want with me. I'm completely at your command. If you didn't know it before, I hope you do now."

His hand was on the edge of the tub, and Abigail threaded her fingers through his and squeezed. She felt odd being the one offering comfort, but knew how tentative his sanity was at the moment. His guilt oozed out of him, so heavy it almost crushed her with its weight.

There was a long pause, and then he said, "It won't happen again. I realize you have no reason to trust me, but in time, I hope you'll be able to."

Niall helped her out of the tub and to their bed. She didn't tell him she already trusted him and that she'd already forgiven him.

Two years later, Abigail gave birth to the future king. He had a dark complexion, raven hair, and brilliant green eyes. Just like his mother.

www.ingramcontent.com/pod-product-compliance
Lightning Source LLC
Chambersburg PA
CBHW030119260626
47156CB00008B/2716